I0623115

INTO THE DARKNESS

VOLUME 1

ETHAN HAYES

FREE REIGN

ISBN 13: 978-1-953462-18-3

Free Reign Publishing, LLC
San Diego, CA

CONTENTS

CHAPTER
ONE

TERRORIZED BY THE RAKE

I HAD my encounter long before the internet was in everyone's house and I never knew what the creature I encountered was called until very recently. I have been terrified by thoughts of this creature and the memory of it my whole life. It was 1982 when I saw it and I was sixteen years old. I have literally never been the same but I learned very quickly not to discuss my encounter with anyone because you lose friends and people start to look at you differently and not in a good way. However, recently I found out that many people in my community, which is the same one I had my encounter in so many years ago, have had some sort of encounter or another with this so-called Rake entity. It's called that because its hands look exactly like the garden tool of the same name. Due to all of the encounters I uncovered in this particular area of Wyoming, I decided to start a support group. It has done wonders for me and not only is the lifelong terror I've felt subsiding, but I now know I'm not crazy and I've met some lifelong friends as well. I was sixteen years old and like most young people that age I decided one night to lie to my parents about staying at a friend's house and instead me and that friend went to a party. Her name was Janine and she and I were best friends. She is one of the first people I lost due to the encounter but not because she thought that I was crazy but quite the opposite in that she saw it too but didn't want to talk about it anymore. She wanted to pretend like we were making it up in our heads but because of the absence of drugs and alcohol, there's no way we were and I refused to subscribe to that theory. Plus, I saw it for much longer than the second or two she did but I'll explain that a little later on. Anyway Janine told her parents she was staying with me and I told mine I was staying with her. It was so much easier back then because nowadays your parents can track your exact location with your cell phone. Back then it was much more dangerous out in the world in general for teenagers because if something happened to you it took longer for people to find out and also, there weren't as many witnesses or cameras everywhere but we did have the benefit of it being much harder, for the most part, to catch us doing bad things.

Janine and I wanted to go to a party we were invited to by the most popular girl in school. We weren't in with that crowd but her best friends told us to meet them at an old abandoned barn that stood randomly in the middle of some dense and creepy woods. It was a small town and most teenagers and adults knew where this one barn was because it seemed to have no business being where it was but also, it's Wyoming and most parties were held outside in the fields or at old barns. It only seemed weird because this girl was so popular and yet we hadn't heard anything about this party. Normally, even though we hadn't ever been invited before, we would have at least known something about it. However, they explained that away and told us they were surprising her for her seventeenth birthday. They told us not to worry about gifts but to just make sure we didn't get there too early and ruin the surprise. They said not to be surprised if everything looked dark when we showed up because just in case the girl happened to drive by the woods and get suspicious, they were making sure everyone parked at a certain spot down the road and in several different nearby fields and also, that they didn't want to alert her early so there would be no lights at first depending on what time we got there. Now, anyone with half a brain could see where this is going and that we were being set up but we were young and wanted so badly to taste popularity that we would have been willing to believe anything at the time. We were apprehensive but excited and we couldn't wait for that night.

Janine's sister said it would cost us gas money for a ride and that solved the issue of where to park. Neither one of us had our own vehicle yet anyway. Janine's parents tended to ask less questions and also, since her sister was giving us a ride, we got ready at her house. Her sister was a pretty decent big sister so we didn't worry about her ratting us out or anything. She couldn't pick us up though and we just figured we could find a ride from someone and eventually sneak back into Janine's house. As long as her parents were asleep they wouldn't ask about it in the morning.

We got to the barn at around 11:30PM because the surprise was being shouted at midnight, or so we were told. We didn't want to be seen in her older sister's beat up old station wagon and so we got dropped off a bit down the road and we had to walk half a mile into the woods on top of the ten minute walk from where her sister left us to where the trail started. There still wasn't anything amiss that we noticed about the alleged party but once we entered those woods and started making our way to the barn we both felt very strange all of a sudden. We both kept feeling like someone was watching us and only then did it dawn on us that something might not be right about this alleged party. We figured we were already there though so we continued on our way, albeit a bit more cautiously at that point. We made it to the barn and everything was dark and quiet but we knew right away that we had been duped. We were heartbroken and angry but worse than that we had absolutely no way of getting home. We did have flashlights because we knew we would have needed them in order to traverse the woods. We had backpacks with our heels in them and everything. We had come prepared for a party and realized we were the losers who never got invited. Janine was scared because we were literally stuck out there and it was too late to walk the mile or so to the nearest house already, let alone by the time we would have gotten there it would have been way too late to knock on someone's door. We decided to see what we could find in the old barn to maybe just try to make ourselves as comfortable as possible until the sun came up and we could maybe walk to that house or hitch a ride some- where to call her sister to come and get us. We were humiliated and both of us were loudly complaining about those girls and all the things we wanted to do to them for revenge. Just then, as we searched the barn, we heard something fall from up in the loft area. We both froze. Immediately we thought of rats and ran out. It wasn't much brighter outside of the barn, despite the light of the moon. We then heard what sounded like footsteps. Both of us immediately thought that someone was there to take a picture of how dumb we were and we started yelling curses into the barn. However, the footsteps quickly stopped and a dragging sound replaced them.

It sounded like someone was dragging something behind them as they walked. It was really creepy and we yelled for whoever it was to cut it out. Then, Janine shined her flashlight right into the middle of the barn. A pale, ghoulish looking creature turned and looked at us. It opened its mouth and a loud groaning sound came out. It then started towards us, its rake-like hands dragging along behind it on the dirt floor. I took it all in as quickly as possible. It had sharp teeth and black eyes that were almost sunken into the back of its head. It was extremely pale, the skin looked sort of rubbery and it was hairless. It had a humanoid body and though I didn't see the feet, I already told you what the hands were like. Janine and I turned to run but it took us a couple of minutes to understand what we were seeing before we did so. She was ahead of me and I kept telling her to please stop and wait for me but she ignored me. The entity caught up to me and grabbed my leg, scratching it as it tried to pull me to the ground. Luckily I slipped out of its grasp fairly quickly and I only ended up with some surface scratches and nothing that went too deep into my skin. I tried kicking at it. It was so grotesque and moaned the whole time it was coming at us. Janine was gone and I didn't know what to do. I took a chance and climbed into a nearby tree as fast as I could, the whole time not knowing if the entity would be able to come up there after me. I wasn't very high up but I was definitely out of its reach. It was about seven feet tall. Lucky for me I had brothers and knew my way around a tree and how to climb them somewhat easily. I ripped my skirt on the way up and ended up throwing my shoes at the creature but I was in one piece and it didn't seem to be able to follow me up there.

I screamed in terror at the top of my lungs. The creature was agitated, I could tell, and it kept circling the tree underneath me and raking its hands and fingernails down the sides of it. I thought for sure it was going to shred the tree somehow and that would be the end of me. It had sharp, yellow stained teeth and the stench coming off of this thing was unimaginable. I was absolutely terrified and I ended up peeing on myself which seemed to make the creature go even more crazy. I guess it was the smell, gross I know but what can I say? Eventually a car drove past, after I had been in the tree for about an hour, and though I yelled and yelled, they must've not been able to hear me. But, they ended up honking their horn, which made the creature take off running. I was hoarse from screaming and my eyes burned from crying and all of the make up I was wearing. This is how I know that it was intelligent because as soon as the car drove off, and like I said it had an extremely loud engine which is the only reason why I was able to hear it in the first place, it came lumbering back out from hiding and resumed its place underneath the tree below me. I screamed and screamed for at least another hour and the creature got more and more agitated. Eventually I heard talking and saw what looked like flashlights in the distance and I started yelling as loudly as I could despite having almost completely lost my voice. It was the police and they said they had gotten a call about screaming in the woods. They asked me what I was doing and I tried to explain but they accused me of being on drugs. I tried to tell them I wasn't but they didn't listen and drove me home. They rang my parent's doorbell in the middle of the night and told them they found me wild eyed and hanging from a tree. They also told my parents I was under the influence of something. I was grounded for an entire month and no one ever believed me.

As for Janine, the little traitor that she was, she ran and ran until she reached the main road and ended up flagging down a car. She made her way home that way, by hitchhiking in the middle of the night. I asked her why she hadn't gone back for me and she looked me right in the eyes and told me she thought that I was dead and that no one would ever find my body and she didn't know what to do. I eventually forgave her but like i said, we grew apart soon after that. It is such a relief to know that I wasn't alone in my encounter and that this entity is

a real creature that stalks around in the woods and terri-
fies and torments human beings. I would be hesitant to
even want to see statistics about how many people go
missing in places where this entity is said to lurk. I have
no doubt that it's responsible for some deaths at least
though what it does with people once it catches them is
something I have never allowed myself to think about.
I'm not going to start now either.

CHAPTER
TWO

A GUEST IN THE BASEMENT

WHEN MY CHILDREN ask me if I know any scary stories, I usually tell them old fairy tales about evil witches and cruel stepmothers. Occasionally, a story about a wicked king or enchanted lakes creeps into my mind. Of course, everything is child-friendly and not too graphic.

Once, they asked me if something scary had happened to me. Whether I had seen an enchanted hut or made the acquaintance of a ghost. Of course, I always say no. How could I tell them about what I had experienced as a teenager in the house where we now lived?

Our house is at the end of an old country road in the middle of the Rocky Mountains. It is not meant to be lived in permanently. It once belonged to a ranger, and my grandfather ended up buying it from the owner to keep it from being torn down. I can't say exactly what prompted him to do so. But this decision meant that we always took a long trip to the Rockys during the school holidays, and my kids didn't have to be confined to a city during the pandemic.

They spent the last few years remote schooling and playing long afternoons in the woods. Bless her heart, my wife had to get along with us three hyperactive chaotic people and hasn't thrown us out of the house once. Usually, she has to fight with us to come inside rather than outside. This led to some interesting arguments.

However, I inherited the house at the end of the country road from my grandfather since my father had died long before him. An accident during a hunting trip, at least that was what my grandfather told me. Whether it all happened at our house or somewhere else, I don't know. I was very young then, and my grandfather helped my mother to raise me.

Being a passionate hunter himself, he spent a lot of time with me in the woods around the house. Over time, I learned every path and stone by heart, which has often saved my life. It wasn't uncommon for me to get lost in the dense rows of trees or deviate from a path my grandfather had told me about.

In addition to all the flora and fauna, I also learned from him to recognize the different animals by their noises and footprints. This is especially important for hunting.

But that's not all he taught me. Sometimes, he would tell me stories of strange encounters when we sat around the campfire at night. Faceless men blending into the shadow of a tree, and people disappearing in a second. And animals that no scientist had cataloged before. He didn't call them by their names, but I thought I knew he meant Skinwalkers and Bigfoots. We read reports about it at school. At the time, I thought these stories were meant to scare us kids so we wouldn't run off on field trips.

Today I'm not so sure anymore. Whatever it is, what it is and conclusions drawn by assumptions are mostly false anyways.

So when my kids ask me if anything scary ever happened to me, I always say no. which is a lie. Because there was something that happened to me that I still don't know exactly how to classify.

It had been the summer holidays, and my grandfather once again took me to the hut to spend the hot weeks there. After all, there were lakes and enough opportunities to keep a wild teenager like me in check. I had made many friends over the years, and we regularly met up at the national park to play together. So it happened that Mike and Paul stayed with me. Their parents wanted to spend some time together, and grand-father had no problem keeping an eye on us.

He made us chop lots of wood and clean up the cabin's yard. We've been busy with that long enough and would be so tired in the evening that we wouldn't lose our minds and come up with anything to get in trouble. And so it was. As soon as the sun disappeared behind the peaks, we had barricaded almost all the side walls of the hut with piles of wood.

My grandfather shouted for us to come to dinner. So my friends stormed into the cabin while I stowed the axes and saws on the porch. I was alone outside, and I can still remember that all of a sudden, the birds fell silent, which made me look up. I knew the birds would give you cues when a predator was nearby, but I couldn't see anything in the creeping darkness.

I was just turning around when a piercing scream sounded behind me. I jumped, so scared that I nearly let the ax fall on my foot. I didn't recognize the noise. It was loud, so sad, angry, and crashing that my heart stopped for a moment.

"Chester, come in!" I heard my grandfather call out. The scream came from behind me again. I rushed into the house on trembling legs, and Grandfather slammed the door behind me and locked it.

"If you hear this sound ever again, you have to run. Do you understand me, boy?" he said with a severe face, and my friends sat pale on the couch and stared at me with wide eyes.

I just nodded and stared at my trembling hands that just wouldn't come to rest.

The scream rang out again, and we stared at each other without a word.

After a long moment of silence, the birds started to sing in the surrounding trees again. Something like calmness came over us, and we felt hungry. Grandfather had cooked us his infamous goulash and even allowed us to have a beer with dinner. I'm unsure if he allowed us to drink because we had suffered such a shock or because we had been so diligent.

But as soon as we sat together and ate and drank, the incident with the scream was forgotten. Grandfather then went to bed early and let the three of us sit together in front of the fireplace. We drank our beer slowly, and when the bottles were empty, we had the clever idea of stealing one or the other from the cellar. After all, Grandfather had drunk his whiskey before falling asleep, and we knew he wouldn't wake up anytime soon.

We were just getting up to sneak into the basement when we heard a faint scratching at one of the windows. We all froze and stared into the silence. Then the knocking started.

Knock. Knock. Knock.

Slowly, evenly. Like someone wanted our attention.

But we didn't dare look around. It sounded almost as if the knocking came from all the windows that belonged to the living room and the kitchen.

"What is that?" asked Mike, the youngest of us.

I had spent many years in the cabin and had never noticed anything like it before. "I have no idea," I breathed. And again, there was a knock.

Knock. Knock. Knock.

Louder this time. Urgent. As if the person in front of the window was getting impatient. But we still didn't dare to look at who or what was knocking on the windows.

"Chester..." Paul whispered as the knocking stopped again. We all sat back down on the floor, trembling, close together. As if the closeness of each other could protect us. "I have no idea what that is. I don't want to look either," I said, rubbing my face with my hands.

We listened to the silence again, steadily expecting the knock to come again. But it was not like that. Instead of a knock on the windows, we heard the scratching. Something scraped against the wooden walls that ran the length of the house. Lips quivering, we followed the sound with our eyes. The scratching circled us, slowly, evenly, as if the creature in front of the house had its eyes on us.

"I guess I don't want any more beers," Paul said, leaning back against the couch, his eyes fixed on the floor. "Neither do I," whispered Mike, hugging Paul's side. I slid down beside them, staring at the wooden floor below, when the scratching suddenly stopped, and a soft squeak sounded that I knew only too well. It was the unmistakable sound of the small door on the side of the house that led to the basement. It used to be the sign that I would get an ice cream cone, as my grandfather used to go through the outside door to the basement when we sat outside and spent the day there.

After the squeak, the scratching sounded again. Beneath us. In the basement. On the ceiling that was the wooden floor we were sitting on.

"Chester, what is that?" Paul asked, and I shuddered as the scratching was right below us. I felt the vibration of the nails scraping the wood in my butt.

"It's right below us," I whispered, and the scratching stopped.

And then there was the growl. Right below us, loud and clear. At first, it seemed like random noises being pounded together. But then, as it got louder, I thought I could make out my grandfather's name. As if the figure wanted to summon him.

There was another roar, deep and throaty, almost desperate, followed by the clinking of glass and metal. Was that a burglar? Maybe a confused hermit who lived in the forest and got something to eat from grandfather occasionally and was angry because grandfather was already asleep?

The three of us sat stiffly next to each other, staring at the floor and wincing with a yelp as something hit the wooden planks. They were visibly trembling beneath us. In front of us. Followed again by the clinking of glass and the scraping of metal that I couldn't place.

And again, the scream that sounded like my grandfather's name.

"Grandpa!" I screamed, and so did my friends. Underlined by the almost painful roar from the basement. Who was down there?

It wasn't ten seconds before my grandfather stood at the living room door with a startled face. He seemed just as shaken as we were when the roaring got louder. Something crashed to the ground in the basement. It almost sounded like the rack of fishing gear my father had lined up neatly against the wall.

"Go to your room," he said quickly. Without asking any questions, we jumped up and rushed into the small room where we would sleep together. Grandfather locked the door behind us, and then it was quiet.

Suddenly the noise from the basement stopped. Nothing more could be heard.

Shivering, we huddled in a corner, holding each other's hands as we held hands.

I don't know how long we sat there. But before we knew it, we were asleep.

Our room door was open the following day, and it smelled like pancakes and fresh bacon. Grandfather greeted us with a big smile and piled our breakfast onto the plates.

"Well, did you guys sleep well?" he asked as if nothing had happened the night before. He looked rested and relaxed, and for a moment, I thought we all had imagined last night's happenings.

I never saw Mike and Paul again after that incident. At first, it started with excuses for why they didn't come over. Then, they stopped replying to my letters at some point, and their parents changed their phone numbers. Grandfather and I never spoke about what happened. The basement looked the same as ever when I inspected it a few days later. Neither broken glass nor fallen shelves greeted me. I was sure at this point that we had just had bad dreams because of the alcohol.

When my grandfather finally died and I inherited the house, I remembered what had happened. And with every day I spent in the cabin with my wife and children, I hoped the creature, that had visited us that night, was long gone.

CHAPTER
THREE

MANTIS IN THE LAKE

WHILE THE JERSEY Devil is the most obvious and well known cryptid in the state it isn't the only one by far. I grew up hearing about legends of the Jersey Devil as I have always lived in the Garden State. Back in 2002 when I had my encounter I looked it up on the internet and was stunned to find that the entity I saw had a name. Now, there are some major differences between what I saw and what is normally reported and I live in a completely different area than where this being is normally seen but at the end of the day I think they're close enough in description to at least be related somehow. Maybe the one I saw has some sort of gene that is even more mutated than the ones in the original reports. I live in Morris County and the regular reports normally center around one part of the woods and a specific lake whereas I saw mine right near my house and in the woods surrounding my own backyard.

I was fifteen years old and decided to go fishing in some woods behind my house. I was only planning on being out there for a little while and didn't bring much gear or anything with me. There were several little fishing boats with their own ores that just sort of always stayed out there near this lake and I still don't know who owned them but whoever it was didn't seem to mind people using them. In fact I always went out on them with my father and my friends. Until, that is, the day I am about to tell you about now. I have seen some fairly strange things in the woods up to that point but they could all have had reasonable explanations. The encounter with the so-called mantis men is a whole different story as there was no mistaking these things for something normal that one sees everyday while out fishing. I went to the tiny boats, put my stuff into one and then headed out to spend a couple of hours fishing. I had no reason to fear the woods and there was nothing about that day to make me think it would be life changing and one where I would remember every single detail for the rest of my life. I threw my line out and waited. I want to cut right to the chase and so I will leave out all of the mundane and somewhat boring details except to say that several times I felt myself hook an extremely heavy and seemingly very large fish. I didn't want to give up on it and figured since I had hooked it at least 5 times that I could catch it eventually. However, it was soon dusk and there was no chance that I could stay out there night fishing. I wasn't prepared and though there were houses sporadically placed all around that particular lake and surrounding wilderness area that had spotlights and other lights to illuminate it all somewhat, it was rather insufficient for my purposes and I decided to pack everything up and get out of there. I didn't want to get home too late.

I started gently rowing the boat back to the shore so I could hike the mile or so through the woods and back to my house. The trails I took connected to my backyard so it was really a very work trail and one I knew well from traversing it so much. However, suddenly it felt like something grabbed my ore and ripped it out of my hands. It went flying through the air and then, very quickly, the second one followed suit. I was without an ore and it had happened so incredibly fast that I honestly not only didn't know what happened but I had no idea as to what it even could have been. I grabbed my flashlight and shined it all around but I didn't see anything at first. I heard gentle splashing coming from behind me and to me it sounded like a large frog splashing from lily pad to lily pad. After listening for a minute or two though I realized it sounded like something much larger than that and I was more pissed off than scared at that point. I was wondering what type of animal would be able to casually and so quickly rip the ores out of my hands, one after the other, and then toss them as far as they had gone. They were thrown clear across the lake and I saw where they landed, somewhat, in the woods beyond it. I looked in front of me about five feet, which is how far I could clearly see, as I tried to row the boat using my hands. The water was shallow enough that I could swim in it if I really needed to with it being only about seven or eight feet deep. I was five foot nine but I didn't want to jump in the water and deal with trying to swim and pull the boat with all of my clothes on and my boots, in the dark. It was looking like that might be what I needed to do though and eventually I was just prolonging the inevitable.

I saw bubbles rising from about five feet in front of me which was about seven feet or so from the shore. I wanted to keep going but it was very obvious that something had been over there and breathing underwater. That was odd because what breathes underwater like that? I mean, the bubbles looked like it was a human being which is why I was immediately concerned. I thought it would make sense if human beings were out there messing with me because of what had happened with the ores and now the bubbles. I couldn't just sit there but I did decide to give it four or five minutes, figuring if it was a human being then they would have to come up for air eventually and I could catch them red handed. However, the bubbles disappeared and that's when I felt something trying to lift the boat from underneath. I thought for sure I had come across a serial killer or something and was about to be his or her next victim. I was terrified and as I felt the boat actually start to lift. That's when I jumped out of it and swam like my life depended on it back to the shore. It took about three minutes and as soon as I was out of the boat and the water fully, the boat went flying over my head and landed about three or four feet in. I couldn't believe it and swam for my life. Once I made it to the shore, and I could have sworn I felt something grabbing at my ankles but I can't be sure, I immediately got away from the lake and turned to look and see what the hell was going on.

I saw enough air bubbles that it looked like there could have been at least three people breathing and I just "knew" that I was as good as dead if I didn't get out of there and fast. I ran to the boat and lifted it up in order to at the very least grab my backpack out of it. I needed it for school the next day and it had some other essentials in it like my music player. I saw it and grabbed it quickly. I don't know why I decided to turn around one more time but when I did I saw something rising up out of the water. The first thing I noticed was that it didn't seem to be swimming and if it was standing then it was at least nine feet tall based on how deep I knew for sure the water was. It moved oddly though and I couldn't be sure. I was too stunned to move even though I knew that I should run but I simply was paralyzed. I don't know either if that was literal or just my shock. The being slowly came towards me and once it exited the water it was about ten feet away from me. It looked like a giant praying mantis. It WAS nine feet tall or more and looked like a human sized version of the insect. It was bipedal and at first it just stared at me. Then, it started to make a clicking noise that was similar to the sounds that some insects actually make but that I don't think praying mantis's make because I thought they were silent insects. I honestly still don't know and the answers online were very mixed when I tried to look it up afterwards. Then three more creatures started to emerge from the water behind the other one that was already on dry land and they all moved in the same awkward way. They all made it to the land and they were all clicking while I just stood there, dumbly staring at them.

I turned and ran and heard the clicking following me. They seemed to fly very clumsily behind me and I even saw one of them crash into a tree head first when I turned around to see where they were, which I did many times. The others seemed to only be able to fly in very short bursts. It was extremely terrifying and I didn't know what they wanted. I wondered if maybe they were female and with me being a male, did they want to eat me? Were they some sort of extraterrestrial who ate humans in general? I didn't know then and I have no clue now because I never saw them again and like I said, the information online about this particular entity is very scarce and uninformative. I ran like the wind and eventually I burst through my back door. Both of my parents were sitting in the kitchen and immediately asked me what was going on. I told them but I must've sounded like a lunatic because they couldn't calm me down enough to understand me. Eventually I gave up trying to explain and went to take a shower. Afterwards I went and told my father what I had seen. He turned pale white but he didn't respond. He simply walked outside on the back deck and lit a cigarette. I went to bed.

The next morning my father drove me to school and on the way he told me he had thought he saw the same exact creatures as what I was describing numerous times when at that lake but he always saw them from enough of a distance that he would be able to convince himself he was merely seeing things. I think that's the problem even nowadays in that human beings don't trust themselves enough. Even now when we know so much more about entities like this one and other cryptids like sasquatch and mothman and dispute the plethora of knowledge we have now about extraterrestrials, we don't want to believe it sometimes. My dad and I went back to that lake several times but never managed to see anything and eventually I moved out and went to college. That was the last time I saw the mantis beings on that land or near that lake. I thought I saw them one other time in some woods in Louisiana but I couldn't be sure. It's all so baffling though because real praying mantises are said to stay away from water. I mean, the whole thing is baffling but it's like the more I research, the more I uncover and the more confusing it all becomes. I don't know what else to say except I still research the subject and have even spoken personally to some of the fishermen from the lake in Hackettstown where they've always been otherwise seen but no one really knows what they actually are and or what their intentions are either. Like with everything else, who knows if we will ever find out the answers we seek with regard to any of it.

CHAPTER
FOUR
BENEATH THE STREETLIGHT

IT WAS A QUIET NIGHT, and the streets were empty. The only sound was the occasional car that rushed by and the flickering of streetlights that illuminated the pavement. I could hear the hum coming from the street lights ahead and the sounds of the pedestrian crossing light as it ticked away the moments before it would change. I had just gotten off from work. I worked the late shift at the local burger joint, just a few blocks from my house. I really enjoyed walking home at night. The air felt lighter then, cooler, and it was easier to breathe. It was the only time I could really be by myself and walking home gave me an opportunity to think. As I walked down the wide sidewalk, I was happy to be heading home from my shift.

Suddenly, like a cold breeze blowing over a new grave, I started to get a weird feeling. I couldn't shake off the feeling of unease that crept up my spine. I felt as if I was being watched, and that's when I saw them - a group of children - down the street standing alone beneath a streetlight. Despite the chill in the air, they didn't seem to feel the cold at all.

I wondered what children were doing out so late at night. Their presence at this hour was unusual, and I couldn't help but wonder what had made them come out. It was normal to see kids out at night, but this gang was different. They looked younger than the usual bunch, and their demeanor was menacing. As I walked past them, I noticed how strange they looked. Their faces were pale, their hair was unkempt, and their eyes were sunken. They wore ratty clothes that looked like they were about to fall apart. They looked like they had come from another era, or maybe another world. Even though their faces were obscured by the shadows, I could feel their eyes piercing through me. They stood there, silently on the corner beneath a streetlight. As soon as I laid eyes on them, a sense of dread washed over me. They looked like they were all between the ages of 6 and 11, and their eyes were completely black. I couldn't see any white or pupils, just blackness.

I wondered what a group of children was doing out so late at night without any adults around. They didn't seem like they were playing or fooling around. They were just standing there, staring. I felt a chill run down my spine, I jaywalked across the street and I started to walk away, hoping they wouldn't follow me.

As I walked away, I could feel their fixated eyes on me piercing through my hoodie and then I heard them starting to walk, taking a step off the curb. Their steps were in sync with mine. I knew that they were following me, but I didn't dare look back. I felt as if they were trying to communicate or intimidate me, but I didn't understand what they were doing or what they were trying to convey.

The group followed me for several blocks, and I started to feel uneasy. I turned around to confront them, but they remained silent and focused, continuing to follow me. I tried to pick up the pace, but they were always walking in my shadow and right behind me. I quickened my gait, but soon I heard the sound of their little footsteps following closely in my footsteps. The black-eyed children were getting closer, and I could hear their breathing. It was heavy and labored, as if they were out of breath.

I turned around to confront them, but they were gone. They had vanished into thin air. I was alone on the empty streets, and the only thing that remained was the flickering of the streetlight overhead and the long shadows that were being cast by the mixture of the streetlights and the bright, full moon.

I couldn't shake off the feeling that I was being

watched, and I felt as if the black-eyed children were still out there somewhere, waiting for me. I wondered if they were real or just a figment of my imagination.

As I reached my street, I glanced over my shoulder. They were gone and I finally breathed a sigh of relief. But relief didn't last long. I turned to cut across the neighbors lawn and I saw them, waiting in front of me, standing beneath another street lamp as I turned the corner. They had somehow managed to get ahead of me, and were now walking towards me.

Their eyes were fixed on me. It was an overpowering feeling and I could feel their presence as if they were standing right next to me. I wondered if they were lost or if they needed help. I stopped and asked them if they were lost, but they didn't respond. They just kept walking towards me, their eyes fixed on mine.

I broke into a very fast speed-walk and began to hurry to my house. I saw them in unison take a step off the sidewalk. They were beginning to head towards me. Silently I began to pray and I hoped that they would turn back and leave me alone. However, they continued to follow me, and their syncopated steps became louder. I could feel my heart pounding in my chest as I reached for my keys and rushed to unlock my door.

As I pushed the door open, I heard their footsteps getting closer. I slammed the door shut and locked it, but I knew that it wouldn't stop them if they really wanted to get in. I rushed to the window to see if they were still out there, but I couldn't see anything in the darkness. Grabbing the curtains, I jerked them closed. I didn't want to see into the night and I didn't want the night to see in to my home.

I tried to shake off the feeling of fear that gripped me, but I couldn't. I felt as if they were still out there, waiting for me to come outside. I really wanted to grab the mail and bring in the trashcans, but that could certainly wait until the morning light.

I decided to take a long hot shower and wash the event off of me. I didn't realize it was going to be an impossible and daunting task. You just can't wash the creep factor off of your skin, no matter how long you stay under the shower.

The night was really busy at the burger joint and I didn't have time to take a break, much less have anything for dinner. Usually I don't eat this late at night, but I knew I needed something to calm my nerves. I had a feeling I wasn't going to be falling asleep anytime soon, so I decided to make something to comfort me. I cracked open a can of tomato soup and made my world famous grilled cheese sandwich. I thought I'd settle in and watch a little late night TV just to calm myself down.

Gathering all the ingredients of my late night buffet, I walked into the front room where the TV was. I still had the feeling that they were out there, so I didn't turn any lights on in the house. Still, there was a blue flickering glow coming from the television which made dancing shadows across the curtains. I looked over to the door, to double check and make sure it was locked. Phew. It was. I decided to put the chain on the door, something I hadn't done in years. *This is ridiculous; I'm an adult and three little kids in old, ratty clothes scared the daylights out of me. I bet they're awesome at Halloween. I wonder if I could rent them for my next party.*

I put my plate on the coffee table in front of the sofa and got up to lock the chain on the door. It was only a few steps and I was at the door in no time. I still had my socks on my feet and the television was turned down low, so I was not making a sound at all.

The chain was dangling down the side of the door frame. I reached for it and just as I touched the chain, there was a knock at the door. A knock at the door? At THIS hour? The knock was very low on the door. I had the feeling that there was a group of creepy little kids outside my door, reaching as high as they could to knock. I wasn't going to fall for that. I wasn't falling for the demonic cookie selling kids. I mean, that's what they were doing. Or so I rationalized. They must be selling cookies… at midnight. *Children are good and they don't hurt people.* Children also do not sell cookies at midnight.

I was frozen in terror, unsure what to do next. If I put the chain on the door, they would hear me. And if I didn't, then I would be afraid that someone was breaking in. Taking a deep breath, I bit the bullet and slid the chain across the door. Again, there was a knocking on the door. I chose to ignore it.

I returned to the TV and began flipping for a movie or something. Finally, I found something I enjoyed and one of my favorite movies. *The Shining* was on. I picked up my sandwich and began to take a bite. Suddenly, from the television I heard *"Danny doesn't live here anymore"*.

"And... we're turning THAT off."

I decided I wasn't very hungry after all, and went to put up my cheesy buffet, then scurried off to bed, locking my bedroom door behind me. The night was long, and I couldn't sleep. Every sound made me jump, and every shadow made me wonder if they were there.

The next day I asked around, but no one had seen any children out alone at night. The entire experience was so bizarre and strange, it made me wonder if what I saw was real or just a nightmare. It was as if they had vanished into thin air. Little did I know, this crazy memory of the black-eyed children standing beneath the streetlight at night was going to be something that remained with me, haunting me for years to come.

I couldn't shake those kids, the way they looked. Why were they following me and where were their parents. I felt like they wanted to harm me, but they were kids. Kids don't hurt people. So why did I feel like they wanted to hurt me? It took a while, but I finally was able to shake the fear and dread that also followed me home that night. I tried to forget about the black-eyed kids following me, chasing me home, but their memory stayed with me. I felt as if they were always watching me, waiting for the right moment to strike. Even though I only lived a few blocks from work, that was the last time I ever walked home at night. From that moment on, I drove to work.

Years passed, and I had moved on with my life. I had a new job and a family, but the memory of that night stayed with me. One day, while I was walking to my car, I saw a group of kids that looked familiar. They wore the same ratty, baggy clothes and had faces so pale they almost glowed in the darkness, their hair was unkempt, and their eyes were sunken. They stood together, shoulder to shoulder, beneath a streetlight. Their eyes were fixated on me. I tried to casually glance at them, to see if it really was the same kids I had seen so many years ago, but they were across the street. As I turned to walk to my car, I heard them. In unison, like they were working as one unit, they stepped off the curb. The gravel under their feet made a sound, and it all came rushing back to me. The memory of that night flooded my mind and I couldn't stop it. Their footsteps were in sync with mine. The sound of their steps echoed in my ears. The terror and horror came flooding back to me like a dam of fear had just broken. I was being washed away and I couldn't stop it.

My heart began to beat wildly in my chest, so hard I thought it was going to explode. I knew that they were the same gang of kids that had followed me that fateful night. They still had the same menacing demeanor, and I felt as if they were waiting for me to turn and look into their black, soulless eyes. I knew if our eyes made contact, that was it for me. I would be gone, gone forever.

CHAPTER
FIVE

THE DEMON OF THE DESERT

I STEPPED onto the desolate plains of West Texas, the dry wind whispering through the tall grasses. The sun was setting, casting an eerie glow over the barren landscape. My heart pounded in my chest as I ventured deeper into the unknown, drawn by the allure of the legend that haunted this desolate region. I scoffed at the notion of the Chupacabra, dismissing it as a mere figment of superstition and folklore. The idea of a bloodsucking creature haunting the depths of the night seemed absurd, nothing more than a tale concocted to terrify the gullible. Yet, a nagging curiosity tugged at the corners of my mind, whispering doubts and challenging my disbelief. What if, against all odds, there was a kernel of truth to the legends? What if, buried within the realm of myth, lay the story of a lifetime?

Reluctantly, I embarked on the journey to investigate

the alleged existence of the Chupacabra. As I delved deeper into the research, my skepticism mingled with a tinge of excitement. The prospect of unearthing the truth, of unraveling a mystery that had captivated the imaginations of countless individuals, ignited a flicker of anticipation within me. If the Chupacabra were real, it would be the ultimate scoop, the pinnacle of my journalistic career.

The chilling tales of the Chupacabra lingered in my mind, sending shivers down my spine.

The air grew heavy with an unexplainable tension as I scanned the horizon, searching for any sign of movement. Shadows danced and twisted in the fading light, playing tricks on my anxious mind. The silence was deafening, broken only by the distant howls of unseen West Texas creatures. A knot of fear tightened in my stomach, warning me of the dangers that lurked in the darkness.

As the last traces of daylight vanished, the landscape transformed into a sinister realm. The once-familiar terrain became a maze of uncertainty and dread. Every rustle of leaves, every distant creak of a tree branch, sent chills racing down my spine. My senses were heightened, hyperaware of the unseen presence that slinked through the night.

A cold gust of wind swept across the desert, carrying with it a bone-chilling feeling. It whispered secrets of the supernatural, a reminder that I had stepped into a realm where reality blended with nightmares. The moon emerged from behind a thick veil of clouds, casting a pale, ghostly light that accentuated the desolation.

As I continued my journey, a feeling of being watched enveloped me. The weight of unseen eyes bore down upon my vulnerable form, and a primal instinct screamed at me to turn back. But my curiosity, tinged with an insatiable thirst for the truth, propelled me forward into the heart of darkness.

With every step, the legends grew louder in my mind. Whispers of bloodthirsty creatures with glowing red eyes and razor-sharp fangs echoed through the recesses of my thoughts. Each gust of wind carried with it the haunting howls that pierced the night, a chilling chorus that sent shivers racing down my spine.

I arrived in the desolation of West Texas, my heart pounding with a mixture of excitement and trepidation. I had always been fascinated by the paranormal, drawn to the mysteries that lurked beyond the veil of our everyday reality. My obsession with the unexplained had driven me to pursue a career as a paranormal investigator, but nothing could have prepared me for what awaited me in this forsaken land.

I stepped out of my vehicle; a gust of wind swept through the barren landscape, whispering secrets of the unknown. My eyes scanned the darkened horizon, taking in the terrain that stretched before me. The silence was oppressive, broken only by the distant howls that sent a shiver down my spine. The very air itself held its breath in anticipation.

I carried with me a lifetime of experiences, a tapestry woven with encounters that defied logic and challenged the boundaries of my understanding. But this was different. The legends of the Chupacabra had followed me like a shadow, haunting my dreams and fueling my determination to unveil the truth. Now, standing in the heart of the land where these stories had originated, I could feel their weight pressing upon me, a heavy burden of expectation and dread.

The locals had warned me of the dangers that lurked in the darkness, their voices laced with a mix of fear and resignation. They spoke of livestock mutilations, unexplained disappearances, and the ever-present threat of the creature. Their words echoed in my mind as I prepared my equipment.

The moon cast an eerie glow on the abandoned plains as night descended, casting long shadows that seemed to dance and twist in the ghostly light. With a deep breath, I stepped forward, my footsteps leaving imprints on the barren ground. As I ventured deeper into the heart of darkness, I knew that this investigation would push me to the limits. The Chupacabra awaited, ready to test the resolve of a mere mortal who dared to challenge the unknown.

I couldn't shake off the feeling of impending doom as I delved into the heart of West Texas, following the trail of clues that led me closer to the enigmatic Chupacabra. The locals spoke of its sinister presence, their eyes filled with a mixture of fear and resignation. Some whispered tales of loved ones who had vanished without a trace, their blood drained from their bodies, leaving behind only a sense of horror and despair.

I reached out to those who had encountered the creature, desperate to unearth any hidden truths. Their stories were chilling, hauntingly similar. A farmer, burdened by the weight of responsibility, told me of his livestock, mercilessly slaughtered and left in disarray. He spoke of the fear that gripped his heart every night, the sound of unearthly howls echoing through his nightmares. His once-thriving livelihood had been reduced to a graveyard of broken dreams.

Another witness, a survivor of a chilling encounter, trembled as he recounted his ordeal. He described glowing red eyes that pierced through the darkness, a feral creature with razor-sharp fangs that had attacked without mercy. The memory of that night was etched into his very soul, leaving behind scars that no amount of time could heal.

Armed with their testimonies, I scoured the desolate

desert for signs of the Chupacabra's presence. The landscape conspired against me, casting long shadows that danced and twisted, distorting reality. Each step felt like a journey into madness, as if the land itself cloaked its secrets hidden from prying eyes.

My equipment, meticulously prepared and tested, crackled with anticipation. Night vision cameras captured the slightest movement, audio recorders stood ready to capture the haunting howls that echoed through the night. Every creaking branch, every rustle of leaves, sent a chill down my spine. I knew the Chupacabra was watching, lurking just beyond the reach of my senses, observing my every move with predatory eyes.

As I followed the trail of mutilated carcasses, I couldn't help but wonder about the creature's origins. Local legends spoke of a curse, a farmer wronged and transformed into a bloodthirsty monster by dark forces. The lines between myth and reality blurred, leaving me trapped in a maze of uncertainty, where nightmares bled into daylight.

With each clue I discovered, the puzzle of the Chupacabra's existence grew more intricate, more terrifying. Footprints, too large to belong to any known creature, pointed towards a cryptid of untold horror. A tuft of fur, matted with blood, hinted at the creature's insatiable thirst for the life force of its victims. The evidence mounted, creating a portrait of a malevolent force that defied reason and defiled all that stood in its path.

As the moon reached its zenith, casting an mystical glow upon the desolate land, I knew I was nearing the heart of the mystery. The air grew thick with an oppressive energy, a palpable sense of foreboding that clung to my skin. Every instinct screamed at me to turn back, to abandon this perilous quest. But I couldn't escape the pull of the unknown, the need to uncover the truth that burned within me like a fevered obsession.

I pressed on, fueled by a mix of fear and determination. The Chupacabra remained elusive, leaving behind only fleeting traces of its presence. Yet, I knew that I was drawing closer to an encounter that would test my limits at every turn. The final clue awaited, somewhere out in the open desert.

The creature eluded me at every turn, its presence a haunting specter that danced just beyond the reach of my senses. I had pursued many elusive creatures throughout my career as a paranormal investigator, but none had evaded capture with such calculated precision. The very essence of the Chupacabra seemed to mock me, to revel in the terror it instilled in its victims.

Every lead I followed led to dead ends, the clues disintegrating like ashes in my grasp. Witnesses spoke of fleeting glimpses, a shadowy figure disappearing into the night with supernatural swiftness. If the Chupacabra was a phantom, it was a shape-shifting entity that defied comprehension. It slipped through the cracks of reality, leaving behind a trail of confusion and fear.

The more I delved into the enigma of its elusiveness, the deeper I descended into a maddening abyss. Every piece of evidence I thought I had discovered was snatched away, replaced by ambiguity and doubt. It was as if the creature reveled in toying with my sanity, luring me further into its labyrinth of terror.

The night turned into a symphony of dread, the darkness becoming a canvas upon which the goat-sucker painted its macabre masterpiece. I could feel its eyes upon me, a malevolent gaze that sent icy fingers down my spine. It watched and waited, testing the limits of my resilience, as if daring me to come closer, to unravel the truth that lay hidden in the depths of its elusiveness.

With each failed attempt to capture the cryptid, the weight of its presence grew heavier upon my shoulders. The creature's elusiveness gnawed at my soul, feeding on my desperation and filling me with an unsettling mixture of fear and fascination. It was a game of predator and prey, and I had unwittingly become the hunted.

As the night grew longer and my obsession with it deepened, my own grip on reality began to falter. Sleep became a battleground, haunted by nightmares that blurred the line between the waking world and the realm of the supernatural.

The desert creature reveled in its elusiveness, leaving me with an insatiable hunger for answers that seemed forever out of reach. Its presence loomed over me, a constant reminder of the terrors that lay hidden in the darkness. The pursuit of the elusive Chupacabra had become a dance with my own demons, an unending nightmare that threatened to consume me whole.

The air grew thick with an unsettling tension as I ventured deep into the heart of the wilderness, following a promising lead that would bring me face to face with the monstrous Chupacabra. The moon hung low in the sky, casting a sickly glow over the landscape, as if the very heavens mourned the impending horror. I could sense its presence, it was out there, lurking just beyond the edge of perception, its malevolence radiating like a vaquero returning from a long dusty trail ride.

As I crept forward, the silence enveloped me like a suffocating shroud. Not even the wind dared to whisper. Nature itself held its breath in anticipation of the impending encounter. Shadows twisted and writhed, casting grotesque silhouettes that danced upon the ground, mocking my faltering resolve.

A rustle of gravel and rocks, too close for comfort, sent a jolt of fear coursing through my veins. I turned, heart pounding in my chest, to find myself face to face with the embodiment of nightmares. The Chupacabra stood before me, its eyes glowing like fiery embers in the darkness. Its feral snarl revealed rows of razor-sharp fangs, dripping with the blood of its victims.

Time stood still as the creature lunged, its movements a blur of supernatural agility. I barely had time to react, my instincts kicking in as I narrowly evaded its deadly assault. Panic surged through me, each heartbeat drumming a desperate rhythm, as I fought to stay one step ahead of the relentless predator.

The encounter unfolded in a grotesque ballet of fear and survival. The Chupacabra's unearthly howls pierced the night, resonating deep within my soul. Its eyes never left me, burning with a vicious intelligence that seemed to revel in my terror. I could feel its hot breath on my neck, a sickly sweet odor that clung to the air like a rancid perfume.

Every move I made, every calculated step, was met with a swift counterattack. The Chupacabra's claws tore through the darkness, leaving deep gashes in the earth as a testament to its deadly prowess. I fought against the rising tide of despair, desperately seeking an opening to strike back at the beast that had become my nemesis.

But in the end, it was the Chupacabra that had the upper hand. Its relentless onslaught wore me down, my strength waning with each passing moment. With a final, bone-chilling shriek, it retreated into the night, leaving me battered and broken, a mere shell of the person I once was. I couldn't help but wonder, why didn't the creature kill me? Why didn't it finish me off? Why leave me broken and wounded? The unearthly encounter had forever etched itself into the deepest recesses of my mind, a haunting reminder of the true horrors that lie hidden in the darkest corners of an unknown existence.

The Chupacabra's wrath descended upon the land like a merciless storm, leaving a trail of destruction in its wake. Its thirst for blood knew no bounds, and I found myself caught in the crosshairs of its insatiable rage. The creature moved with an unearthly grace, a nightmarish blend of speed and precision that defied comprehension.

As the moon bathed the desolate landscape in an abnormal glow, I witnessed the true extent of the Chupacabra's wrath. Its eyes burned with an unholy fire, a demonic light that held the promise of pain and suffering. The air reeked of death, the scent of fresh blood mingling with the stench of fear. It prowled the night, leaving behind a gruesome tableau of mutilated bodies and shattered lives.

The creature struck with ruthless efficiency, its victims unable to comprehend the horror that descended upon them. Livestock lay in disarray, their throats torn open with brutal precision, their life force drained. The once-thriving farms transformed into scenes of carnage and despair, as if an evil force had been unleashed upon the unsuspecting.

I witnessed firsthand the aftermath of the cryptid's wrath, the grisly remnants of its voracious appetite. Bloodstained fields stretched out before me, a testament to the creature's insidious power. It showed no mercy, no remorse, as it reveled in the havoc it wrought. My faith in the natural order had been shattered by the sheer magnitude of its maliciousness.

The Chupacabra's wrath extended beyond mere physical violence. It struck at the heart of the human spirit, preying upon our deepest fears and darkest secrets. Its presence was a constant reminder of our vulnerability, a stark realization that we were but helpless pawns in a game of supernatural forces.

The fury of the creature lingered long after its physical presence had faded into the night. Its haunting cries echoed throughout my mind, a reminder of the terror I had witnessed. Its supernatural outrage had left an indelible mark upon the land, etching the chilling legacy of the creature into the collective memory of those who had dared to face its unholy temper.

The unyielding mystery of the West Texas Cryptid enveloped my every waking thought, gnawing at the edges of my sanity. No matter how many clues I uncovered or witnesses I interviewed, the truth remained frustratingly out of reach. The creature defied all attempts at classification, its origins shrouded in a veil of darkness that refused to be lifted. It was a riddle that taunted me, a puzzle with pieces that refused to fit together.

The more I delved into the enigma, the deeper I descended into a labyrinth of uncertainty. The creature's very existence seemed to challenge the laws of nature, defying scientific explanation and rational comprehension. It was a creature of myth and nightmare, a macabre paradox that lurked in the shadows, always just out of grasp.

The mystery of this goat-sucking demon haunted my dreams, its elusive nature fueled my obsession. I scoured ancient texts and folklore, seeking answers in forgotten tales and whispered legends. But the more I learned, the more I realized that the true nature of the cryptid eluded even the most seasoned investigators. It was a force beyond comprehension, a supernatural riddle that dared to exist outside the realm of human understanding. And in its mysterious presence, I felt the weight of an eternal nightmare, the unsettling realization that some secrets were never meant to be revealed.

I had ventured deep into the darkness, peered into the abyss, and faced the ultimate truth. I was a witness to the creature's presence, saw how it hung heavy in the air. Its menacing aura suffocated every breath, like it relished the fear it instilled in its pursuers.

With dismay coursing through my veins, I now stood

at the precipice, reflecting upon my final confrontation. There was no hiding from the truth. The moon cast a pale glow upon the desolate landscape, illuminating the grotesque tableau of carnage that lay in its wake. The Chupacabra's wrath had left an mark upon the land, a haunting reminder of the horrors it had wrought. Stepping forward, the world around me seemed to warp and contort, twisting into nightmarish shapes that defied reason. The very fabric of reality trembled under the weight of the Chupacabra's presence. Shadows danced and writhed, mocking my faltering courage, as if the darkness itself had come alive to witness the impending horror I was forced to face.

I then realized, in the climax of our devilish dance, I glimpsed the true nature of the creature, the emptiness that lurked behind its eyes. It was a void, devoid of hope and sanity. Its final blow struck true, my world faded to black, and I realized that the true horror lay not in the creature itself, but in the knowledge that its insidious presence would forever haunt me. Never knowing why it did not kill me but instead it chose to run off - that's a fear that I will always live with. The Chupacabra's reign of terror would endure, an eternal nightmare from which there was no escape.

PUBLISHER'S EXCERPT 1

I SAW BIGFOOT

SOUTH CAROLINA SIGHTING

So, I'm not really sure about the exact order of things that happened, but let me know if you think this is weird or not. I never realized what one of these things were until I started listening to your podcast a few years ago. I emailed you a while back, but I didn't share all of my experiences that happened at my childhood home where my mom still lives.

So, I grew up in Marion, SC. It's a tiny town about an hour away from Myrtle Beach. Population's around 6 thousand, and it's spread out. Mom's still out there in the country. Back then, we had two houses on our right, and one across the road from us, opposite a few fields. Country life, you know? To the left and behind our place, there were just fields for miles. Depending on the season, it'd be corn, soybeans, or tobacco. I got two older sisters, and we all lived in this small home with a barn-like thing we called the boat shed. Dad kept his boats, lawnmower, and stuff like that there. In our backyard, we had this big oak tree, and this massive magnolia tree in the front. Funny thing is, mom actually grew up on that land and moved back after she got married and had us.

We used to have these "prowler" issues, as my parents would say. Banging on windows, things going missing from the boat shed, and these "people" peeking into our windows. Now, let me tell you about one time. I was probably around 10 years old, and I had this major fear of the dark – whole different story why – and my big sis asked if I could spend a night in her room. My other sis and I shared bunk beds in another room, and we were super tight, like best buds. Me and the older sis, we had our moments, you know? She could be real mean, but sometimes she'd surprise me with some kindness. Should've been suspicious, really. So, I thought it was cool she was asking me to crash in her room, even though I was kinda scared of her.

Anyway, her room was like pitch black, only light was this red glow from her digital clock on the dresser. So, there we are, in our PJs, and she's telling me to get into bed. This bed's shoved in a corner, so you can only get in from one side. I crawl in, heart already racing 'cause I'm thinking, "What's she up to?" She's being weirdly nice, saying not to be scared, that she'll hold my hand till I fall asleep. I'm thinking she's planning something, like smothering me or something, LOL. So, we're lying there, it's a decently comfy bed, and she kills the light. I'm lying there, feeling better 'cause I can see a bit from the light coming through the blinds. She's like, "It's all good, I'm right here." I'm like, "Fine, whatever." I'm not sure why she's acting so chill, but it's late, and my eyes are getting used to the dark and the tiny bit of light.

I start drifting off, not sure how long I was out, but suddenly, I hear tapping. Even as I type this now, I'm feeling exactly how I felt that night, like 40 years later! I'm just looking around with my eyes, frozen with fear. I don't know why I'm so scared, 'cause I don't know what the sound is. I move my arm under the covers to feel if my sister's there, and yep, she's there, fast asleep. The tapping's coming from the window and it's getting louder and louder. I shift my eyes over, not moving my head, and I see this HUGE dark figure blocking most of the window. I'm holding my breath, feet freezing, realizing that's fear, right? I'm petrified. I think these "prowlers" are trying to break in. The blinds are kinda slanted down, so lying there, I can see a bit of whatever it is. All I can make out is that it's black and has these super white teeth. A big ol' mouthful of 'em, and I can hear it breathing, all raspy and gurgly.

I grab my sister's arm, whisper-shout, "Someone's at the window." She's like, "What?" I say, "Someone's trying to get in!" Trying not to move, talking real low. She shouts, "What?" I scream, "Someone's trying to get in!" She looks, sees the figure, and bolts out of the room, screaming for Dad. I slide out of bed, don't look back 'til I hit the floor, then crawl outta there faster than lightning. "Dad, Dad, someone's trying to get in the window! Hurry!" Now, Mom and Dad are asleep, but Dad jumps up when we scream, grabs his .38 revolver – yeah, he had that thing for dealing with these "prowlers" – and dashes out the front door in his underwear. Mom calls the neighbors, they grab their guns too and go help Dad. Mom's convinced they're gonna accidentally shoot each other, but that's Dad. He comes back in a bit, saying he heard 'em running through the tobacco field, saw a dark figure breaking the stalks, but couldn't see details. And just like that, we're supposed to go back to bed like it's all normal. Yeah, right. I'm in the living room, sis goes back to bed, parents too.

I'm glued to the TV the whole dang night, totally freaked. I can still see it now, like I'm there. Can still hear it. Do I know what that thing was? Nope. But listening to your episodes where people talk about hooded folks or mysterious figures, it all comes rushing back. So, about a year ago, I went back to Mom's. Listened to some more of your guests' stories, talked to Mom – Dad's gone, passed away six years back – but Mom's still holding strong at 84, got my nephew with her, so she's not alone. She's got a load of stories from that house, which I'll share someday. Went back to that window where that "person" was ages ago, measured it up. No bricks or flower beds under there, just the hedges that were always there. The window's bottom is at 5 feet, and that thing took up the whole dang window!

So, I'm guessing it was like 7 and a half, maybe 8 feet tall, unless whoever it was had a ladder or something. Me and Mom just stood there, totally amazed. How did we just think that was a regular person? It hit me like a ton of bricks! Told a few close friends, got the "You're crazy" look and a grin, so I let it be. But I can't. The more I think about all the wild stuff that happened out there, something was going on, man.

———

I SAW BIGFOOT: BOOK 1

PUBLISHER'S EXCERPT 2

13 PAST MIDNIGHT: VOLUME 1

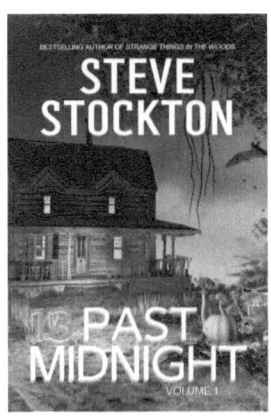

The Terror of Elmsworth Forest

I've always been drawn to the mysterious and eerie. By age five, I was immersed in tales of the supernatural, much to my parents' amusement. They would chuckle and shield my eyes during the spooky scenes.

Throughout school, I took a filmmaking class where each project I presented had an eerie twist, so much so that my teacher once commented that I should explore other genres. The reason I share this background is to emphasize my unquenchable thirst for the supernatural, a thirst that would lead me to a spine-chilling experience I'd never forget.

In Elmsworth, a town I grew up in, whispered tales spoke of an age-old sorceress who once roamed our forests. Legend has it that she placed a curse on Elmsworth's land after being executed in the 1700s. Although many towns boasted similar tales, our legend was fortified by old documents I stumbled upon in our local library during the late 90s, long before online searches were commonplace.

In my mid-twenties, with a gap year before university and a casual job at my aunt's store, I had time to spare. Emboldened by these findings, I decided to venture into Elmsworth Forest, hoping to encounter this legendary sorceress. While my friends declined the invite, citing concerns about the forest's restricted access, my then-girlfriend, although not a fan of anything spooky, suggested I remain respectful if I attempted any spiritual communication.

In those times, our knowledge of spiritual mediums was limited. Ouija boards, marketed as amusing board games, were easily accessible, so I took one with me into the forest. To avoid detection, a friend dropped me at a trailhead after sunset, planning to pick me up at dawn.

The forest's foreboding atmosphere intensified as night deepened. Setting up camp, I eagerly awaited midnight, the supposed witching hour. Lighting a solitary candle, I placed my fingers on the Ouija board's planchette. Instantaneously, it hurtled across the board, spelling "LEAVE" repeatedly. Before I could react, it ended with a haunting message: "you belong here" and abruptly moved to "Goodbye". The candle extinguished. An oppressive sensation gripped me, and distant screams echoed eerily.

Frantically, I packed the board and ventured down a trail, attempting to distance myself. But those harrowing screams persisted. The ominous sensation intensified, and at one point, I awoke from a terrifying dream to find myself face to face with a ghastly figure.

She floated eerily, her sagging, ancient face mere inches from mine. With grotesquely angled neck and predatory eyes, she was the embodiment of horror. Her image matched the library sketches of the sorceress of yore. Around her, shadowy figures lurked, their presence felt more than seen. A primal fear consumed me. I bolted, leaving my belongings, the shadow entities and the sorceress pursuing relentlessly.

Reaching the road bordering the forest, it became evident she couldn't cross, confined by some ancient rule or curse. She watched from the trees as I hitched a ride home, her sinister shadow companions' red eyes piercing through the night.

Days later, visiting the library, I confirmed her resemblance with the sorceress in the sketches. That nightmarish ordeal forever distanced me from the supernatural. The shadow entities seem to have followed me from the forest, appearing occasionally in my life. Dreams of that night still haunt me, serving as a chilling reminder of the dangers lurking in the unknown. If sharing my tale deters even one person from meddling with forces beyond our understanding, then it's worth recounting.

———

13 PAST MIDNIGHT

CHAPTER
SIX
FORGOTTEN SHADOWS

IN THE EERIE depths of that old Victorian house on Sycamore Street, where shadows whispered untold secrets, I, a staunch skeptic, found myself entangled in a paranormal web. Stephen King once said, "The trust of the innocent is the liar's most useful tool." Never had those words held more weight than when I moved into that dark and dusty house. What started as a last choice became a descent into a nightmarish realm, blurring the line between the living and the dead. As I set foot inside, little did I know that the house's dark past and restless spirits would challenge my disbelief and force me to confront the inexplicable.

The first night alone in the house was an exercise in endurance, a trial by darkness. The air was thick with an otherworldly chill, seeping into my bones like icy tendrils. The creaking floorboards echoed through the silent halls, an unsettling symphony of age and neglect. I stood at the threshold of the unknown, my heart pounding in my chest like a trapped animal.

As dusk surrendered to the cloak of night, the house came alive with eerie whispers and phantom footsteps. Shadows danced on the peeling wallpaper, contorting into grotesque shapes that seemed to taunt my fragile sanity. The flickering candlelight cast dancing shadows that clawed at the edges of my vision, playing tricks on my senses. Every sound, every creak, sent shivers down my spine, as if unseen eyes watched my every move. The house held its secrets close, its walls heavy with a history that pulsed like a dormant heartbeat. Sleep eluded me, and I found myself ensnared in a waking nightmare, where reality melded with the twisted fabric of the supernatural. It was a night of torment, a dance with the macabre, and I knew that my journey into the depths of that haunted house had only just begun.

The nights in that house were suffocating, weighing with an otherworldly presence that lingered in every corner. I thought the days would be better, so I began opening every curtain that shrouded a window. They were heavy and filled with dust. Opening the windows would let fresh air flow through, so I began to open them all. That's when I first heard it. The whispering voices that crept into my dreams, their sinister tones seeping into the very fabric of my being, were alive and in the room with me.

I could still hear them from the night before, the remnants of their haunting words still echoing in my ears. *It's just the wind*, I told myself.

Deciding I needed a cup of tea, I walked into the kitchen and flipped on the light switch. The lights, those damnable flickering lights that danced like malevolent specters, taunting my fragile sanity, created shadows on the kitchen walls. Reaching back and touching the switch, I quickly flipped them off.

Enough. I was beginning to have enough. I ventured deeper into the house. Sunlight filtered through the cracked windows, casting an ethereal glow on the worn floorboards. It was in this silence, amidst the lingering scent of aged wood and faded memories, that I heard them again, the voices. Whispers carried on an unseen breeze, their spectral tones reaching out from the depths of the house. They spoke in hushed murmurs, their words a cryptic symphony that sent a chill down my spine.

As I followed the disembodied whispers, the air grew heavy, charged with an otherworldly energy. The house trembled with a supernatural force, and I watched in awe as objects began to stir, defying the laws of nature. Books began to fly off the shelves, their pages rustling in protest, while chairs scraped across the floor as if guided by invisible hands. It was as if the house itself had come alive, a stage for the unseen forces that held sway over its desolate existence.

My heart raced, caught between terror and fascination, as I witnessed this macabre spectacle. Shadows danced on the walls, twisting and contorting into grotesque forms that seemed to mock my very presence. The whispers grew louder, their words intertwining in a chorus of anguish and despair. In that moment, the line between the living and the dead blurred, and I found myself an unwilling spectator to a paranormal performance that defied comprehension.

In the midst of this supernatural symphony, a sense of unease settled upon me. I could feel their presence, the entities that lingered in the house, their ghostly forms shifting in and out of my peripheral vision. The room became a battlefield between the tangible and the ethereal, a clash of realms that threatened to tear the very fabric of my reality. Fear gripped me, but curiosity held me in its relentless grip, compelling me to bear witness to the extraordinary.

With every passing moment, the paranormal occurrences grew stronger. The voices grew louder, their words now a chorus of desperate pleas and mournful cries. Objects continued to move with purpose, their invisible puppeteers seemingly driven by a malevolent force. I stood rooted to the spot, an unwitting spectator in a realm where the laws of the living were rendered obsolete. In that haunted Victorian house, I had entered a realm where the veil between the worlds was thin, where the echoes of the past reverberated with an intensity that defied explanation.

But amidst the terror, there was an insatiable curiosity that gnawed at me, pushing me to unravel the mystery that lay within those haunted walls. I was determined to find a rational explanation, to prove that it was all a figment of my overactive imagination. Yet, deep down, a part of me knew that I was only fooling myself. There was something inherently unnatural in the way the atmosphere thickened, in the way my skin prickled with each unexplained occurrence. Skepticism began to crumble, brick by brick, until all that remained was a shaky belief in the paranormal.

I decided to go into town, check out the library and see if there were any books or newspapers on the history of the house or on the family I did not know.

It was a short walk. No one was inside. Why should they be? This is the age of Google. Just google it. I was different. I wanted the book in my hand, I wanted to feel the weight of history as I turned each page.

The metal door was heavy, feeling like it had not been opened in ages. There, behind a large desk, sat the librarian. Quietly I walked over and asked the reference librarian for help, casually mentioning the subject of my research. She pointed me to a section, filled with dusty volumes of the local newspaper. Maybe I would find the answer that I needed.

With a feeling of unease and an insatiable need for answers, I ventured into the forgotten depths of the library, determined to uncover the secrets that bound the haunted Victorian house. Dusty books and yellowed newspapers adorned the shelves, each holding a piece of the puzzle that had eluded me for so long. Fingers trembling, I delicately retrieved a stack of old newspapers and settled into a worn armchair, ready to delve into the dark history that shrouded my residence.

My hands began to tremble, my heart filled with fear. I embarked on a journey into the forgotten past of the house. I delved into dusty archives, sifting through faded documents that spoke of lives lived and lost. And there, buried amidst the pages of forgotten history, I uncovered a dark secret that tied the restless spirits to their eternal torment. It was a tale of betrayal, of tragic love turned sour, and the echoes of those tortured souls still reverberated through the very foundations of the house.

As I perused the brittle pages, the air grew heavy with anticipation, as if the spirits of the past leaned in, eager to share their long-held secrets. It was there, among the faded ink and smudged print, that the truth revealed itself; the house had been the site of a chilling murder-suicide. The articles painted a haunting picture of a once seemingly idyllic family torn apart by the depths of human despair.

According to the reports, a family had resided in the house decades ago. Thomas, a troubled artist with a tormented soul; Elizabeth, his fragile and devoted wife; and their young daughter, Emily, whose innocence belied the darkness that lurked within their home. Thomas, consumed by demons that only he could see, had succumbed to madness, ultimately turning his twisted desires towards his own family. In a fit of horrific rage, he had taken the lives of Elizabeth and Emily before taking his own, forever staining the walls of the house with the weight of unspeakable tragedy.

The newspaper clippings chronicled the aftermath of the murder-suicide - the shocked neighbors, the police investigation, and the whispers that lingered in the town's collective consciousness. It was a story of shattered dreams, of lives abruptly cut short in a spiral of anguish and despair. The house, once a sanctuary, had become a tomb, its rooms forever tainted by the echoes of that fateful night.

As I read those chilling accounts, a mixture of sorrow and terror washed over me. The weight of the past bore down upon my shoulders, intertwining my fate with that of the ill-fated family. The presence of the spirits became more tangible, their mournful whispers seeping through the cracks in the walls, pleading for acknowledgment, for redemption. The house was a mausoleum, and I had unwittingly become its custodian, bound to confront the restless souls and unveil the truth that had remained buried for far too long.

As I pieced together the fragments of the past, I couldn't help but feel a strange connection to those spirits. Their pain, their anguish, seemed to seep into my very soul, intertwining our fates in a macabre dance. The skepticism that once held me captive had been replaced by an all-encompassing curiosity, a desire to understand their plight and, perhaps, offer them some semblance of peace. But little did I know that the confrontation with the spirits would be just the beginning of a battle for survival, a battle against the forces of the supernatural that threatened to consume me whole.

Without realizing it, I spent the entire day within the walls of the brick library. It was time for me to leave and I barely scratched the surface. As I cautiously stepped into the dimly lit foyer of my new home, a chill ran down my spine, signaling that something had changed within the Victorian house. The air hung heavy with anticipation, pregnant with a spectral presence that seemed to permeate every inch of the space. It was in that eerie stillness that I caught a glimpse of her - Emily, the innocent victim of the house's tragic history. Her ethereal form stood before me, her eyes brimming with a mixture of fear and longing. I had stumbled upon a bond that transcended the boundaries of life and death.

Emily's presence radiated an unspoken plea for understanding, for solace in a realm that had held her captive for far too long. Instinctively, I extended a trembling hand, offering comfort in the face of her spectral existence. I whispered soothing words, assuring her that she was no longer alone, that she need not fear the darkness that had claimed her. It was a delicate dance of trust, a fragile bridge between the living and the dead.

Together, we explored the house, room by room, exorcising the lingering shadows that had tormented Emily's restless spirit. I guided her through the hallways, dispelling the echoes of her untimely demise. We unraveled the memories that held her captive, allowing her to confront the pain that had shackled her to the house for so long. With each step, Emily's essence grew brighter, her spirit lightened by the release of her haunting past.

As days turned into nights, Emily began to shed her fears, finding solace in my presence and the newfound understanding of her plight. We laughed amidst the echoing halls, banishing the lingering gloom that had pervaded the house for years. I became her confidant, her protector in this spectral journey. Together, we carved a path towards healing, weaving a tapestry of hope amidst the darkness

In the final moments of our shared journey, I looked

into Emily's eyes, filled with a bittersweet mixture of sorrow and hope. The time had come for her to let go, to move forward and embrace the peace that had eluded her for so long. With a tender voice, I assured her that she had faced her demons, that it was safe to release the shackles of her past. She had found the strength within herself to transcend the confines of the haunted house, to seek a realm where joy and serenity reigned supreme.

With a trembling smile, Emily nodded, a newfound radiance illuminating her ethereal form. She knew that she was no longer bound to the haunting memories that had tethered her to the house. It was time for her to journey towards the light, to embrace the infinite possibilities that lay beyond the realm of the living. I reassured her that she need not be afraid, that her spirit would soar to heights unimagined, free from the chains of her tragic past. It was a farewell suffused with both sadness and hope, as we bid each other farewell, our souls forever connected by the bond we had forged.

As Emily's essence dissipated into the ether, a profound stillness settled over the house, as if the very walls exhaled a collective sigh of relief. The weight of the past lifted, leaving behind a sense of renewal and liberation. No longer burdened by the echoes of tragedy, the haunted Victorian house began to reclaim its lost vitality. It stood as a testament to the resilience of the human spirit, and a reminder that even in the face of darkness, there is always a glimmer of light that can guide us towards redemption.

And so, Emily departed, leaving behind a legacy of courage and the imprint of her ethereal presence. The house stood transformed, its atmosphere lighter, infused with a newfound serenity. It was as if the spirits of the past had found their peace, carried away on the winds of change. The haunted Victorian house, once a place of torment, had become a sanctuary, a sanctuary where Emily's spirit would forever linger, a beacon of hope and a testament to the power of letting go.

CHAPTER
SEVEN

THE LIGHTHOUSE OF BAYCLIFF

AS THE COLD wind whipped through my hair and the salty scent of the ocean filled my nose, I found myself standing before the towering sentinel that was the Lighthouse of Baycliff. Its weathered exterior bore witness to years of relentless storms and unforgiving waves, a testament to its endurance against the elements. Little did I know that stepping foot inside this imposing structure would immerse me in a chilling tale of lost souls and tragic fate.

I remember visiting once on a school trip, walking the land were the lighthouse has watched the ocean for so many years. Even then, the whispers of the land being haunted were prevalent. The locals spoke of ghosts, of voices carried by the wind, and of strange apparitions emerging from the mist. It was as if the land itself was cursed, and no one could escape its grip. As I explored the area, I couldn't shake off the feeling that something was amiss. It was as if an invisible force was watching my every move, following me, and waiting for the right moment to strike.

I couldn't believe my luck when I won the prize of a night alone in the lighthouse. For years, I had been fascinated by legends of its haunting, and I couldn't wait to investigate it for myself. As I made my way up the winding staircase, every step creaking beneath my feet, I could feel my heart racing with anticipation. The historical society had left me with a warning to not go wandering in the dark and to be careful, but I was determined to uncover its secrets, no matter the cost.

The journey to the lighthouse was treacherous, the jagged cliffs and crashing waves serving as an ominous prelude to the haunting that awaited. As I stepped inside, a shiver ran down my spine, for the air was thick with a presence that could not be ignored. The flickering candlelight cast eerie shadows on the peeling wallpaper, as if the souls of the lost were caught in a perpetual dance. I ventured deeper, guided by an intangible force that drew me closer to what I believed to be the heart of the haunting.

The room I would be staying in was small and damp, with a single bed and a desk. The walls were lined with old books and maps, and an old-fashioned lantern sat on the desk. As the sun began to set, I prepared myself for a night of exploration. The light from the lantern flickered eerily as I made my way down the stairs and into the dark, foreboding night. I must had been in the room where the original lightkeeper, John Westly, lived. How lonely and cold it must have been, staying here alone after the tragic death of his wife, Mary. Placing himself in a self-imposed prison, the lightkeeper had taken an oath that no other shall be driven mad by this land, by this lighthouse. The lightkeeper incarcerated himself to the lighthouse, serving a life sentence for allowing Mary to stay with him, for allowing Mary to be driven insane, That thought stayed in the back of my mind as I began to set up my equipment. REM pods were positioned at the door, alerting me if anyone entered.

I began walking through the interior, the tragic past of the lighthouse gradually unfolded before me, revealing a tale of anguish and despair. Decades ago, the seas that surrounded the lighthouse had claimed countless lives, their ships shattered against the unforgiving rocks. The light that was meant to guide them to safety had become a false promise, a malevolent beacon that led them to their watery graves. Evidently, the lighthouse had become a memorial, haunted by the anguished spirits of those lost at sea.

Each room within the lighthouse held a tragic story. The keeper, a solitary figure bound to his post, had lived a life consumed by guilt. It was said that, overwrought by his grief, he had failed to tend to the light on a stormy night, dooming a ship and its crew to a watery demise. His tortured soul had become forever entwined with the haunted structure, his presence a constant reminder of the price paid for his negligence. As I explored further, I encountered the ghosts of sailors and passengers, their spectral forms forever trapped within the walls, their mournful cries echoing through the halls.

Continuing on, I found a small room. In the heart of the lighthouse, a hidden chamber held the remnants of a forgotten journal, its pages yellowed with age. It revealed the tales of the lost souls, their hopes and dreams drowned in the relentless sea. Their voices resonated within me, whispering of a desire for redemption, for peace amidst their eternal torment. The lighthouse had become a vessel for their restless spirits, a place where the past and present converged in a haunting symphony of sorrow.

I'll preface this by saying that I've always been a non-believer when it comes to the paranormal, but my EVP session at the lighthouse changed everything. As the sun began to set, I set up my equipment - a digital recorder, a spirit box, and a flashlight - and began my session. At first, there was nothing but silence. But as I began to ask questions into the darkness, I heard something that made my blood run cold.

At first, it was just a whisper, a faint voice that I could

barely make out. But as I listened more closely, the voice became clearer, and I heard it say my name. I was alone in the lighthouse, so the voice couldn't have come from anyone else. I was convinced that I had made contact with the other side.

But it wasn't just my digital recorder that was going off. The spirit box was also active, with voices coming through that seemed to respond to my questions. And then there was the REM pod that was set up downstairs at the door. It began to go off repeatedly, with lights flashing and beeps echoing through the empty corridors of the lighthouse.

I tried to remain calm, but the fear was palpable. There was something in the lighthouse with me, and it was with me in ways that I couldn't explain. I felt like I was being watched, like every move I made was being scrutinized by unseen eyes. It was as if the spirits of those who had perished at sea reached out to me, to make contact with the living.

As the night went on, the equipment continued to go off sporadically, with voices coming through the spirit box that sent a chill down my spine. The name John echoed through my paranormal equipment repeatedly, like an insistent plea from beyond the grave. The voice was old and hoarse, strained with agony and despair. As I listened, I could sense that this was not just any John. This was *the* John, the original lighthouse keeper, the man who had seen the worst of the tragedies that plagued the lighthouse.

In my mind's eye, I could see him standing on the shore, helpless as he watched a ship crash upon the rocks, the cries of the dying echoing in his ears. I could feel his despair, his hopelessness as he realized that he was powerless to save them. And even as the spirits of the dead seemed to call out to him, he remained trapped in his grief, unable to let go of the past.

It was then that I realized John's spirit was still trapped in the lighthouse, unable to move on from the pain and the tragedy that had plagued his life. And as his name continued to echo through the spirit box, I knew that I had to help him find peace, to set his spirit free from the haunting that had kept him trapped for so long. The lighthouse had claimed so many lives, but it seemed that the spirits of the dead were not the only ones who were trapped within its walls.

Communicating with the ghost of the lighthouse keeper was an experience that I'll never forget. As his name continued to echo through my paranormal equipment, I began to ask him questions, hoping to get some answers. It was then that I felt a presence in the room, a sense of someone watching me from just beyond the veil of the living.

As I spoke to John, I could sense his sadness and his despair. He had been trapped in the lighthouse for so long, unable to move on from the grief that had consumed him since his wife's death. But when I told him that he could move to the light, that he could finally find peace and rest, John said no. He told me that he wanted to stay in the lighthouse, to keep watch over the living and protect them from the same fate, the insanity, that taken his beloved Mary.

Confused by his actions, I was unsure why he would want to remain trapped in the lighthouse. But as I listened to his voice, I could hear the determination, the conviction in his words. John had made a vow to protect the living, and he intended to keep it, even if it meant staying in the lighthouse for eternity.

As the night wore on, I promised John that I would return with more options, that I would find a way to help him find peace. I gathered my equipment and made my way out of the damp room, still shaken by the experience of communicating with a ghost.

As I stepped into the light of the new day, I realized that the haunting of the lighthouse was far from over. John's spirit still lingered within its walls, and the ghosts of the dead still called out to the living. But I knew that I couldn't rest until I had found a way to free them, to help them find the peace that had eluded them for so long.

As I left the haunted lighthouse, the weight of its tragic past clung to me like a lingering specter. The souls that dwelled within its confines had etched their stories into my very being. Their presence was a reminder of the fragility of life and the unforgiving power of the sea. The haunted lighthouse stood as a testament to the human spirit, forever bound to the ghosts of the past, and forever whispering their tales to those brave enough to listen.

In the days and weeks that followed, I researched every possible way to help John and the other spirits move on. But it was as if the lighthouse had a life of its own, holding on to the ghosts of the dead and refusing to let them go. I knew that the road ahead would be long and treacherous, but I was determined to find a way to set their spirits free. The lighthouse had claimed too many lives, and it was time for the ghosts of the past to finally find peace.

CHAPTER
EIGHT
HORRIFYING FACELESS CREATURE

I GREW up in Arkansas and I lived basically in the middle of the woods. I don't mean to sound cliche because I read a lot of these encounter stories because I am always searching for answers to what I saw and I know that most of them start like that. It's true though and I think that has a lot to do with why I saw what I did. I feel like the forests and woods of the world are places where there are lines between realms and dimensions and sometimes things cross from one to another, whether on purpose or accidentally. Most of the time I don't think anyone notices but I believe that when human beings end up coming across something like what I saw, something unexplainable, that's one of the reasons why. We simply see something we shouldn't have and are then left to live the rest of our lives with that information and most of the time we have no idea what to even do with it all. I was seven years old and was camping in some woods by my house with my mom, dad and older sister. We went camping several times a year, usually with the change of the seasons and it never got boring or old for us. It was the nineteen sixties and there wasn't a lot to do otherwise. Not if you didn't have a lot of money anyway and my family definitely fit under that category. Now, I want to say right here and now that, as strange as it may sound, this was only the first of four times I saw something similar to what I'm about to describe to you. It came in a different guise every time and while this encounter was with "a little girl" it wasn't always that way. It did always happen in the same place though, this one patch of dense woods about a mile away from my grandparent's house. They lived a twenty minute drive from me and my parents and we visited with them a lot. I don't pretend to know what it all means but I wonder if I was chosen or, like I just said, if I just happened to be in the wrong place at the wrong time.

We left my grandparents house in the middle of the day. We had our campervan all packed up and ready to go. We didn't camp in tents anymore because my mom said my sister and I always had a really hard time when we would have to do it that way. I guess we didn't like lying in the dirt or whatever but she never really elaborated and simply said it made her job easier. We were familiar with the woods and spent a lot of time in the ones surrounding our house too. It was scary at night, I remember always feeling like something or someone was watching us. It was the first year we were using the campervan and my sister and I were very excited. We thought it was really fancy and didn't even want to leave it once we parked it in our campsite. My dad was an avid outdoorsman and wanted my sister and I to learn how to survive out there but I think he was giving in to my mom with the rental van. The first night there passed fairly normal and we were all in bed by eleven that night. The next day my mom asked my sister and I if we wanted to go and pick some berries with her. I eagerly said that I did but my sister had already agreed to go fishing with my dad. My mom grabbed some larger bushel baskets and we headed out on our way. We all agreed to meet back at the van in four hours in order to have lunch. Mom gave me my basket and told me not to stray too far away from her. I always wandered off as a kid. I liked to explore and while my parents encouraged that, my mother liked to always have her eyes on me. We picked berries for about an hour and suddenly I was really tired. My mom told me to sit on a large rock and stay with the bushels we had already almost filled while she went and just finished collecting enough berries to fill her last basket. I agreed to stay there and off she went.

My mom still swears she had only been gone ten minutes but in my memory she had been gone for so long I started to get really worried. I yelled out for her but she didn't answer me and so I screamed out to her but still received no answer. I had just started crying when I heard a noise coming from behind me. I heard giggling and turned around just in time to see a little girl in a white dress running away from me. I could only see her back but she had been wearing an old fashioned dress, even for the time it was then, and she had long, dark brown pigtails in her hair. They were braided. I ran after her and she continued to giggle and run deeper into the woods. The fact that I had told my mother I wouldn't move didn't even cross my mind. I was only seven years old and thought that I had found a new playmate. It didn't occur to my young brain that there shouldn't have been another unsupervised child out there, especially not one who was wearing a dress and who had such seemingly perfect hair. I yelled out to the little girl but she didn't turn around and after I chased her for almost five whole minutes, she turned a bend and seemed to have disappeared. I was confused but even worse than that I realized I had gotten lost while chasing her. I stood still and looked all around me but the woods looked a little different. How they looked different I couldn't quite put my finger on but the colors almost seemed brighter while the previously bright and sunny sky had gotten very dark. There were gray clouds in the sky and this only elevated my fear and confusion. I called out for my mother but again received no answer so I yelled for the little girl to come out. I had become convinced she was hiding from me. Just as I turned and started to walk the other way, I heard her giggling again. It was coming from behind one of the trees nearby. I ran over there and saw the same girl, on her knees and facing the tree. Her hands looked like they were in a praying position. I tapped her on the shoulder but she didn't even seem to know I was there. She didn't acknowledge me.

I was very annoyed and mad at the time because she had gotten me lost and then she was ignoring me. I grabbed her shoulder to try and get her to turn around and face me but it was the worst mistake of my life. She did turn around then but when she did I saw that she had no face. It wasn't like there were holes where her eyes and nose should've been but it just looked like nothing. Someone else who has encountered this same type of terrifying entity described it as looking like someone stretched a piece of fabric over a football. It was terrifying and I stumbled backwards and screamed. I was on my behind then and the little girl suddenly stood up. She was about five feet tall, so taller than I was, and she had white skin. Her arms were extremely long and her hands, while otherwise looking normal, hung down to her ankles. She took two steps towards me and stopped again as I tried to scoot back on my behind to get away from her. I didn't have enough room to stand up yet and also, my legs were far too shaky to even try to get up and get away. Then, as I screamed, the little girl turned her head to one side as though she were just staring at me and was very confused. All of this would have been enough but it got worse. She then started to mumble, as though she were trying to talk but her mouth was covered. It wasn't that it was covered so much that it wasn't there and I didn't know what to do. Finally, I couldn't take anymore and I got up to run. I heard the girl mumbling louder and incessantly as she followed behind me. She never ran but she walked very fast. It started to rain and I started to cry. I turned around to see if she was still chasing me and she was. I turned back around to watch where I was going so I didn't fall again and I slammed right into my father. He and my sister were making their way back from fishing. I screamed and fought with my dad to let me go before I realized who he was. He grabbed me and asked me what in the world I was doing. I snapped out of it.

I immediately looked behind me again but there was no one there. She had just been there a second ago and I realized too that it wasn't raining anymore. Not only that, I wasn't wet at all and it was almost as though it had never rained in the first place. I frantically tried to tell my dad and sister what had just happened to me. My sister thought I was just trying to scare her but my father looked more concerned than anything else. He asked me where my mother was and I told him I didn't know. We went back to the camp but my mom wasn't there either and we were in the middle of trying to figure out where we should go to try and find her when she came running through the woods. The minute she saw all of us she looked instantly relieved and ran over to me. She had tears in her eyes and it was like she couldn't believe what she was seeing. I tried once again to tell everyone what happened but none of them believed me. It turned out I had traveled nearly two miles from where we were berry picking to the area where my sister and father had been fishing. I had done that in a matter of mere minutes. Four and a half hours had passed which means I lost about two hours of time that I still have no memory of to this very day. My mom said she never went and didn't hear me far enough that she wouldn't have been able to hear me calling her at all. I got in a lot of trouble and wasn't allowed to participate in any of the fun activities with my dad and sister the whole next day. I had to stay in the campervan with my mom because they thought I had simply not listened to them and wandered off. However, none of them could explain how I had gotten so far in such a short amount of time, but I really don't think that they wanted to. It was all too much for them to handle.

I often wonder if I was abducted or something that day. The other three times I saw a similar faceless entity I also lost time, have no memory of what happened during the missing time and I had always seemed to travel much further than I should have been able to when looking for whatever image the entity presented itself as. I say that because I certainly don't believe I was dealing with an actual little girl, for obvious reasons. I think whatever lurked underneath the guise was pure evil and acted as some sort of lure. Whatever the reason and whomever the entities are, it all felt extremely nefarious to me from the moment I realized I was lost that first time. I don't talk about this in my private life or publicly and aside from trying to tell my parents and my sister that one time on the first day that it all happened, no one knows what happened to me. The other encounters happened throughout different times in my life. The second time I was a teenager and the other two times I was an adult already. It makes no rational sense, I know that, but there isn't anything to explain any of it otherwise either. It was terrifying and the implications of the distances traveled in such a short time in woodland areas I am usually very familiar with in general and the missing time are absolutely horrifying. I don't know if I was chosen or if I randomly stumbled upon the phenomenon and the powers that be, the ones who make these encounters possible and maybe even the ones behind the faceless entities, decided I was a good candidate for further experiences with them. It's all very confusing, I know, but that's really all there is to this particular encounter.

CHAPTER
NINE
THE NEPHILIM

I STOOD in the scorching desert heat, beads of sweat trickling down my forehead and evaporating before they had a chance to cool me. The relentless sun beat down upon the arid landscape, casting long shadows that danced across the barren ground. The air was dry, a parched breath that seemed to sap the moisture from my very being. I shifted uncomfortably from foot to foot, my patience tested as I waited for the bus to arrive. The minutes stretched on, each passing second magnified by the sweltering surroundings. The desert seemed to hold its breath, the stillness broken only by the distant hum of cicadas and the occasional gust of hot wind that stirred the sand. I yearned for the respite of shade, for the relief of air conditioning, as the minutes turned to an eternity in the relentless desert heat. I gathered with a select few hand-picked students, the brightest of the department, to go on the journey of a lifetime.

The unblinking sun cast harsh shadows upon the desolate landscape, its unforgiving rays reflecting off the sandy terrain. This was where my journey began, a summer dig that would forever change the course of my life.

As a college intern, I had been granted the opportunity of a lifetime to assist the world-renowned archaeologist, Dr. Benjamin Carter, in unraveling the mysteries of the past. But little did I know that this excavation would lead me down a path of dark discoveries and unfathomable truths. We were in search of something greater than ourselves. We were searching for the elusive and legendary Nephilim.

My fascination with the Nephilim had haunted me since childhood. These legendary beings, spoken of in ancient texts and whispered in hushed tones, were said to be the offspring of celestial beings and mortal women. Towering in stature and possessed of fiery red hair, they were a hybrid race, a mingling of gods and humans.

I was a tall teenage girl with fiery red hair that cascaded down my back like a waterfall of flame. It was a feature that both fascinated and drew attention, making me stand out from the crowd. But with my height and vibrant locks came the taunts and whispers of my peers. They would jeer and tease, labeling me as a

Nephilim, a descendant of the mythical beings spoken of in ancient tales. Their words stung, each one a reminder of my perceived otherness. Yet, amidst the mockery, there was a glimmer of defiance within me. I embraced my uniqueness, refusing to let their words diminish my spirit. For deep down, I knew that being called a Nephilim was not an insult, but a testament to the extraordinary possibilities that lay within me.

Legends painted these ancient giants as mighty warriors, endowed with supernatural abilities and blessed with immortality. They were a link between realms, straddling the line between divinity and humanity. But these tales were dismissed as mere myth and folklore by the skeptics, consigned to the realms of fantasy and imagination.

The notion that the Nephilim were not simply mythical beings but extraterrestrial entities left on Earth is a tantalizing possibility that sent a cold chill down my back. What if that was part of my history, part of my DNA? It's not like I could send in a cheek-swab and compare the bloodline between myself and a biblical giant.

As I delved deeper into the ancient texts and pieced together fragments of forgotten lore, a new narrative emerged, one that hinted at celestial origins and a connection to otherworldly realms. The Nephilim, with their towering stature and fiery red hair, defied the boundaries of human existence, their presence on Earth a testament to a cosmic intervention.

I pondered the implications of this revelation, allowing my mind to wander into the depths of speculative possibilities. Could it be that these celestial beings were stranded here, their advanced technology lost or dormant, awaiting discovery? Were they sent as emissaries from distant planets or civilizations, tasked with shaping the destiny of humanity? Or were they banished by their own, to this planet, to live out their lives until they ceased to exist? The very thought made my blood run cold for a moment; it meant that our understanding of human history and our place in the universe was about to be forever altered.

As I went deeper into the mysteries of the Nephilim, a question gnawed at the recesses of my mind: Why were they stranded on Earth? What cataclysmic event had marooned these celestial beings on our humble planet? The very thought filled me with fear, for it hinted at forces beyond our comprehension, cosmic machinations that shaped the destiny of the universe itself. And it begged an even more ominous question: If there were Nephilim on Earth, could there be more scattered among the stars, waiting for the day when they would reclaim their celestial birthright? Would they descend upon our world with awe-inspiring power and unimaginable purpose? The mere contemplation of such a possibility filled me with both fascination and dread, for the secrets of the universe were vast, and the presence of the Nephilim on Earth was just the tip of an unfathomable cosmic iceberg.

The more I delved into the annals of history, the more convinced I became that the Nephilim were not mere figments of ancient storytelling. There were fragments of evidence scattered throughout the texts, fragments that hinted at a profound truth waiting to be uncovered.

And so, when the opportunity arose to join Dr. Carter on his desert excavation, I seized it without hesitation. It was a chance to delve into the depths of history, to unlock the secrets that lay hidden beneath the sun-baked dunes. Little did I know the horrors that awaited me in that arid expanse.

Dr. Benjamin Carter, a figure shrouded in a cloak of enigma, cast a long and foreboding shadow upon the world of archaeology. His appearance was as weathered as the ancient artifacts he so fervently sought, his face etched with the lines of countless hours spent beneath the unforgiving sun. His piercing eyes, framed by bushy eyebrows, seemed to hold the weight of forgotten civilizations, as if they had gazed upon truths that would drive lesser men to madness. His graying hair, unkempt and windswept, mirrored the chaotic nature of his relentless pursuit of knowledge. Dr. Carter was a man of few words, yet his presence spoke volumes - an imposing figure who commanded respect and inspired both awe and trepidation. His countenance, simultaneously marked by weariness and unquenchable determination, hinted at a lifetime of unyielding dedication, where the pursuit of truth surpassed personal comforts and delved into the realms of obsession. He was a figure revered in the world of archaeology, a man of graying hair and weathered features. He had spent his life unearthing the mysteries of the past, driven by an insatiable curiosity that matched my own. But behind his esteemed facade, he carried a personal burden - a sister lost to an unexplained illness, her life extinguished before her time.

In his grief and desperation, he turned to the ancient texts, searching for answers, for solace. And within those dusty tomes, he stumbled upon references to the Nephilim, the celestial beings whose existence had fascinated and eluded humanity for centuries. The tales spoke of their extraordinary abilities, their connection to the divine, and their seemingly immortal nature.

The discovery ignited a fire within Dr. Carter, a fire that burned with equal parts obsession and hope. He dedicated his life to unraveling the enigma of the Nephilim, seeking to find answers that transcended the realm of science and medicine. And I, in my youthful fervor, became his willing companion on this perilous journey.

Our excavation site stretched before us, a desolate

patch of desert marked only by a cluster of tents and scattered tools. With each swing of the pickaxe, each sweep of the brush, we unearthed fragments of a forgotten era. The dig site yielded a treasure trove of artifacts that defied the boundaries of time and beckoned to a forgotten era. Ancient relics, clay shards, ancient tools, and faded hieroglyphs emerged from the sand, like whispers from the past, their weathered surfaces whispering tales of civilizations long gone. Exquisite pottery, adorned with intricate patterns, bore witness to the skilled hands of artisans who had once shaped them. Fragments of stone tablets, inscribed with cryptic symbols, held the keys to deciphering the secrets of the past. And the discovery of ancient weaponry, rusted but still imbued with an air of lethal power, hinted at a tumultuous history of conflict and conquest. Each artifact was a tantalizing piece of the puzzle, offering glimpses into the lives of those who had come before. A chorus of voices from the distant past, calling out to be heard and understood.

Days turned into weeks, as the blistering sun beat down upon us, testing our resolve. We toiled tirelessly, our hands calloused and our bodies weary, driven by an insatiable thirst for discovery. And then, on a day when the sun blazed high overhead, I made a discovery that would forever change the course of our excavation.

Half-buried beneath the shifting sands, I unearthed a

bone. It was large, weathered, and unmistakably human. But it was not just any bone. It was colossal in size, defying the bounds of what we believed possible. And clinging to its surface were strands of fiery red hair, the hallmark of the Nephilim.

I called out to Dr. Carter, my voice trembling with a mixture of excitement and trepidation. He rushed to my side, his eyes widening as they fell upon the bone. It was a relic of the Nephilim, a tangible piece of evidence that took our breath and captured our imaginations.

Amongst the bones of the Nephilim, we unearthed a cache of artifacts. The grave, it seemed, held more than just the remains of these mythical beings. There were trinkets and talismans, carefully placed with a purpose that eluded us. Glinting amulets, adorned with symbols of unknown origin, hinted at ancient rituals and a belief system that transcended human comprehension. Curiously, we discovered a small, intricately carved figurine, a depiction of a celestial being, perhaps a deity worshipped by the Nephilim themselves. Its presence suggested a profound connection between these beings and forces beyond our understanding.

But it was the discovery of a weathered tome, its pages brittle with age, that seized our attention. The script inscribed within was a language lost to time, but we sensed its significance. As we painstakingly translated its contents, the words unraveled a tapestry of forbidden knowledge, woven by a civilization on the cusp of both divinity and downfall. It spoke of cosmic gateways, celestial alignments, and dimensions beyond our own. The bones of the Nephilim were not simply the remains of mighty beings, but keys to unlocking a deeper understanding of existence itself. The artifacts buried alongside them were touchstones to an unimaginable realm, a realm where gods and monsters danced a macabre tango, and the boundaries of reality were blurred.

In that moment, the weight of our discovery settled upon us. The implications were staggering, the Nephilim, the mythical beings of ancient lore, had indeed walked the earth. It was a revelation that could shake the foundations of history, challenge established beliefs, and unleash a storm of controversy.

But as we stood there, the bone cradled in my trembling hands, a sense of unease crept over us. We found ourselves standing on the precipice of a decision, should we share this discovery with the world, or should we keep it hidden, safeguarding its secrets from those who might exploit them?

Doubts and fears swirled within us, like the sands whipped up by the desert wind. We contemplated the ethical implications, the potential for chaos and upheaval that such knowledge could unleash. And in the end, we made a choice, an uneasy alliance between truth and secrecy.

We would reveal our discovery to a select few, an inner circle of scholars and experts who shared our passion and dedication. Together, we would sift through the evidence, analyze its implications, and prepare a narrative that would challenge the boundaries of human understanding.

News of our discovery spread like wildfire through the academic community, igniting fervent debates and capturing the imaginations of scholars and enthusiasts alike. The once-silent desert canyon transformed into a bustling hub of activity, as experts and curious minds flocked to witness the unfolding of history.

Dr. Carter's career ascended to new heights, his dedication and tireless pursuit of knowledge vindicated. And I, the young intern whose fingertips had brushed against the bones of the Nephilim, found myself thrust into a world that surpassed my wildest dreams.

Media outlets clamored for interviews, eager to hear my firsthand account of the discovery. I became a reluctant figurehead, thrust into the spotlight with a responsibility that weighed heavily upon my shoulders. The once-quiet student had become a symbol, a vessel of knowledge and revelation.

As the sun rose, painting the desert sky with hues of pink and gold, I stood on the shifting sand of the desert, watching its ascent with a new sense of purpose. The horizon stretched before me, a canvas of endless possibilities. The weight of the Nephilim's legacy rested upon my shoulders, but instead of burdening me, it propelled me forward.

With each sunrise, as the world awakened to the truths we had unearthed, my resolve grew stronger. The desert whispered its secrets to me, its ancient winds carrying the echoes of forgotten civilizations. And as I walked alongside Dr. Carter, our footsteps etching a path through the sand, I knew that we had played our part in rewriting the annals of history.

But the story of the Nephilim was not just a tale of bones and legends. It was a tale of the indomitable human spirit, the unyielding pursuit of truth that defied all odds. It was a reminder that the answers to life's greatest mysteries often lay hidden beneath the layers of time, waiting for those brave enough to seek them.

Within the sands of time and the echoes of ancient ruins, the story of the Nephilim remained, waiting for those who dared to peel back the veil of secrecy. Driven by a hunger for knowledge and a thirst for the extraordinary, we continued our quest, ready to confront the mysteries that lay hidden beneath the desert's ancient embrace. Humanity isn't ready to give up the comfort they find in believing what they have been told. Little sheep in the pen, so many do not want to explore the "what if" of life and are content to stay in their small part of the field, doing as they have been told. But there is an awakening of souls who want to know more, who want to understand and it is for those I continue on in my search for the hidden truth.

The sun still illuminates our path, casting long shadows upon the shifting sands. For those of us who are steeped in the mystery teachings we are beginning to step forward unafraid, into a future where the extraordinary mingled with the realm of possibility, forever altering the trajectory of human understanding.

Next stop? Göbekli Tepe!

MY ENCOUNTER STARTS off fairly simple in that I wanted to know more about some experiences I had been having since I was young with something I couldn't explain. This was back in the nineteen seventies when things like cryptids and spirits, extraterrestrials and other so-called mythical and mystical entities weren't really publicly discussed. My obsession with the supernatural and all of the beings and creatures that go along with it started when I was only twelve years old and saw what I know now was a sasquatch, on more than one occasion, in my yard and the surrounding woods. I didn't know what it was that I had seen but I somehow knew as soon as I laid eyes on it that I wasn't supposed to have seen it. No one believed me and that upset me because I knew what I saw. I had spent a lot of time at the library in my hometown doing tons of research and reading everything I could get my hands on about such creatures and entities and the one thing I kept seeing was that most of these so-called monsters were most often spotted in Alaska. I couldn't very well up and move to Alaska as a preteen but I knew I had a mission for when I was old enough to do so. That may have been the end of it and it probably would have died as nothing more than an old and unfulfilled dream but I started hearing strange sounds and seeing other strange phenomena and entities as well in my hometown in Louisiana. I knew I had to figure out if creatures like sasquatch and others really did exist. I did the right thing and went to school and started interviewing people right out of college about experiences they've had with creatures and beings similar to a lot of the ones I had been seeing most of my life in my own backyard. That area of Louisiana is known today as a hotbed of activity and many of the things I had seen have been sighted by many others too. Before I knew it I had a post office box where people from all over the place would send me their encounters and I would call them up and interview them. It was completely done by word of mouth and a lot of the time it was just someone hoaxing me but I was very satisfied by the hobby. When I was twenty six my parents both died tragically and suddenly and my life went into a downward spiral. My engagement had fallen apart and so I took the money I inherited and decided to take a time out from life and head to the last frontier. I made some calls and got in touch with some of my contacts and was able to rent a small cabin in the middle of nowhere in Alaska. I left as soon as I could and I've never looked back.

The cabin was furnished when I moved in and that was good because I didn't really own any furniture. I hadn't stayed in any one place long enough to have acquired any at that point. I loved the cabin despite its tiny size because there wasn't a neighbor for miles and I was quite literally surrounded by woods. I would hike through the woods daily, despite the snow and bitter cold temperatures, simply to take photos and hope I could lay the cryptid hunting to rest if I could only find some sort of evidence that at the very least bigfoot existed. I was about to get way more than I bargained for. The second Sunday I was there I had gone on my usual hike through the woods and I decided to take a trail I hadn't previously been on. I felt strange from the very beginning because this particular trail seemed to carry with it an air of foreboding and danger. However, I hadn't seen anything on any of the other trails so far so I felt like I had nothing to lose by hiking it. The whole time I walked along the trails and paths, I felt like I was being watched. I also felt like I was in some sort of danger. I eventually came to a surprising sight when I saw a ramshackle, one room shack in the middle of nowhere. Now, I thought where I had been staying was in the middle of nowhere but that place was even more out of the way. It looked abandoned and was missing half of its roof. Someone had cared enough about it though to hang a tarp over the top in order to protect it from the brutal weather. Though every inch of my being was telling me to turn around and never go back that way again, my curiosity got the better of me and I approached the shack.

I called out for anyone who may have been inside and when I received no answer I decided to look in the windows. There weren't that many of them, I think there were only four, and I soon realized that all of them had been covered with dark black sheets or something. I couldn't see inside and it was frustrating. I wanted to ask whoever it belonged to if they had ever seen anything strange out there but there seemed to be no one home. I walked up to the front door and as a last ditch effort I knocked. I didn't expect anyone to answer and no one did but I suddenly heard the sound of running and whatever it was came right up to the door. It was some sort of animal and it was snarling and growling; barking at the door. I figured it was just the owner of the place's dog. However, suddenly the door in front of me started shaking as the animal behind it started slamming itself into it. It was trying to get to me, whatever it was, and by the way the door was moving and from all the sounds I was hearing, it was much bigger than your average pet canine. I decided to leave well enough alone and get back home before it started getting dark outside. I turned and quickly got out of there but I could hear the beast shaking the door and slamming into it, as well as the incessant barking and growling, for a while as I walked the trails back home. It freaked me out and I wondered what sort of animal could move a door like that. I didn't know enough to consider myself lucky I had gotten out of there in one piece. I was though.

I finally made it back to my cabin with just a few moments to spare before the sun went down fully. I took a shower, changed my clothes and then made myself some dinner. I couldn't shake the feeling of being watched and it was intensifying as the night wore on. I was almost in a state of absolute panic by the time midnight rolled around. I checked to make sure the windows and door were locked for the tenth time that night and then I went to the back bedroom to go to sleep for the night. I was hoping to wake up feeling better because I could barely contain myself as far as the fear and panic that seemed to be gripping me for no reason at all. I laid down and the clock next to my bed said it was half past midnight. I started to doze off but was jolted awake by the sounds of howling coming from the woods around my house. It was really scary because it sounded like it was extremely close. It also sounded a little off when compared to how I knew wolves sounded in the wilderness. After not hearing anything for a few minutes I laid back down in my bed to try and get back to sleep. All the lights were off in the cabin but the light of the full moon shined into the curtainless windows of my bedroom made it easier to see my bedroom door. I remember I kept staring at it and couldn't keep my eyes closed. I suddenly started hearing what sounded like something scratching all along the sides of the cabin. I could hear nails digging into the wood and it sounded like it started on one side and ended on the other. I heard it as it went past my bedroom window, just below where the pane ended and met the wood. I was scared but at first I was just hoping that whatever it was would go away without me having to get up and go see what it was out the window.

Though the scratching noises eventually stopped, I was awake in my bed and highly alert. I kept listening and heard what sounded like something breathing heavily. It sounded like it was coming from right outside and underneath the one window in my bedroom that was closest to my bed. I got up and crept over to the window to look and I saw a gigantic wolf. It looked normal enough except that it was standing on all fours and was still about five feet tall. I was taken aback at first but decided to ignore it. It didn't make sense that a wolf would have been able to go all around the cabin and scratch along the sides of it but nothing was making much sense at that time because I was so exhausted. I went to lay back down but then the wolf howled loudly and I thought I'd better go over and throw something at it and try to shoo it away. I thought meat would coax it at least to leave me alone and I honestly had no idea why it was so close to my house or why it was alone. I thought better of feeding it and just opened the window and yelled at it. It didn't budge and just stared at me. I yelled and cursed at it but it did no good. Then, something terrifying happened. The wolf fell to the ground and looked like it was having a seizure or something. It was howling and groaning in pain and twisted all over the place. I could hear what sounded like bones cracking and possibly even breaking and though I couldn't see all of what was happening, the sounds were enough to terrify me into just wanting to make it all stop. That lasted for a minute or two before finally the groans started to sound like a human being was in pain and no longer like it was an animal. Then, it went still and was silent. I could barely make it out because it had moved further away from the window in the fit it had been having. Then, just when I thought that it was dead and wondered what I was going to do about that, if anything, it stood up.

When it stood up I swear it was more man than wolf. It had a human chest that looked extremely ripped and physically fit but it still had the face and head of a wolf, along with the ears. The tail was gone and it had somehow sprouted legs and arms as well. It stood then, as a human, at the very inhuman height of ten feet tall. I was shocked but too scared to even back away from the window at that point. It looked like it was grinning at me and it stood between two trees, just staring at me. The eyes had initially been those of a wolf and looked like they belonged on the animal but now its eyes were more human than anything else and they looked almost amused then as I just stood there staring at it. It leaned against the tree and snarled at me. Then it got down on all fours and something just told me to get away from the window. I ran to the door but then decided I better not leave the bedroom. I think there was a part of me that thought I was having some sort of lucid dream or nightmare. I stood at the door, turned around and watched as the top of its head was visible as it crashed into the side of the house. I heard it whimper and then it growled and snarled again. I inched closer to the window and that's when the previously yellow and glowing eyes had turned red and it was peering through my window at me. It was snarling and howling and its gigantic hands/paws were next to its face in order for it to be better able to see inside of my room. It growled and tried smashing its head into the glass and while the glass seemed like it should have broken it didn't. I started to pray on my knees and I don't know how long I was doing that before I once again looked up. The creature wasn't at the window anymore. I hesitantly made my way over to the window and looked out. I saw footprints in the snow leading away from my house and I also saw blood under the window and the patch of disturbed snow from where it had transformed. I ran to the front of the cabin and looked out the window and sure enough there were wolf tracks or prints leading from the woods and up to my cabin. I laid in bed but didn't sleep again until the sun came up.

I woke up later in the afternoon and that's when I started making the connection between the ramshackle old shack and the werewolf that had been at my cabin the night before. I mentioned it to the man who was renting the cabin to me when he came to collect my rent a few weeks later and he didn't seem to be surprised at all at what I was telling him. In fact, he told me he specifically had reinforced glass installed in all of the windows because he had many encounters of his own with what we both thought was the same creature I had been confronted with that night. I couldn't believe it and this opened up a whole new world for me as far as believing in not only cryptids but also other so-called supernatural entities who I now know are shapeshifters and exist all over the world. That's it for this encounter but I've got a bunch more I can't wait to put out there so stay tuned.

CHAPTER
ELEVEN
GOLD COINS

AS A YOUNG GIRL, I depended on tips from the local diner to support my family. My father had fought in Vietnam and was currently struggling with PTSD, making it difficult for him to work.

I remember the first time I saw my father have a flashback. We were watching a war movie together. Suddenly, he jumped up from the couch, his eyes wild and panicked. He started yelling and thrashing around, reliving some terrible memory from his time in Vietnam.

I was scared and didn't know what to do. But my mother was there to calm him down and bring him back to reality. She told me that my father had been through a lot in the war and that sometimes he had these flash-backs that made him feel like he was back there again.

As I grew older, I learned more about my father's struggles with PTSD. He would often have nightmares and wake up screaming in the middle of the night. And during the day, he would drink beer to numb the pain and try to forget about his past.

Before long my mother could no longer handle his outbursts and she packed her bags. She told me it was my choice to stay or move out now that I was eighteen. I took that moment and looked at my father in the next room. He had his head in his hands and he was crying. I couldn't leave my father. Not when he needed love and understanding the most.

If I worked hard enough I could support us both and afford to get him extra help. I hated seeing my father suffer like this, but I didn't know how to help him. I knew he wasn't the same man that left for war but he was still my father. I couldn't blame my mother for leaving but I couldn't help but feel as if she was abandoning me in the process. She packed her bags that night and we never spoke again. I think she was disappointed that I didn't leave with her or go to college instead.

I wondered if she had found someone new. She didn't think I noticed, but slowly our liquor cabinet had dwindled to next to nothing. Daddy didn't touch the hard stuff. But I didn't have enough time or energy to deal with the hurt I now felt from her absence.

And then one night, everything got from bad to worse.

I came home from my double shift at the diner to find

our family home destroyed. Dishes were shattered, chairs overturned, and garbage was strewn all over the floor. At first, I thought there had been a break-in or a robbery. But then I found my father crying under the table.

I walked into my kitchen, and the first thing that hit me was the overwhelming smell. It was a mixture of spoiled food, garbage, and cleaning products. The sight before me was even worse - dishes were shattered, chairs overturned, and garbage was strewn all over the floor. It was clear that my father had lost control during a terrible flashback.

He was shaking and sobbing uncontrollably, and I knew something was terribly wrong. I sat down next to him and put my arms around him, trying to comfort him as best I could. He told me that he had had a terrible flashback earlier that night. He had lost control and destroyed everything in the house. He was afraid that one day he would hurt me or my mother and that he had become a disappointment to us both.

My heart broke for my father at that moment. I knew that he needed help, but I didn't know how to give it to him. And then I remembered something my mother had told me years ago - that therapy could help people with PTSD.

After I got my father calmed down, I convinced him to take a shower and I returned to the kitchen. I could barely stand the smell. It was musty and moldy, and it made me feel sick to my stomach. I knew that I had to do something to clean up the mess and get rid of the smell.

I started by opening all the windows to let in fresh air. Then I began to pick up the garbage and put it in trash bags. As I worked, I could feel the cleaning products stinging my nose and making me cough. It took hours to clean up the mess, but eventually, the kitchen started to look and smell better. I used a disinfectant spray to clean all surfaces thoroughly and threw out any spoiled food or garbage.

Even after all that cleaning, there was still a lingering smell in the air. It wasn't as overpowering as before, but it was still there. I knew that it would take some time for the smell to completely go away. After hours of cleaning and scrubbing, the smell finally started to dissipate. I managed to talk my father into going to bed to rest.

It was a relief to finally be able to breathe normally again and not be overwhelmed by the stench. It was a difficult experience, but it taught me the importance of taking care of my mental health and seeking help when needed. And it also taught me how to deal with unpleasant smells in a practical way. One part cleaning commercials and two parts old wives' tales helped me whip the kitchen back into shape. I wasn't looking forward to replacing the dishes.

Something had to change before he ended up

hurting one of us. I resolved to start an extra savings fund from my tips at the diner to put my father into therapy. I knew it would be expensive, but I was determined to do whatever it took to help my father. I believed in him and want to give him a better tomorrow.

The money I earned from waiting tables helped with getting my father back on track, and I was so grateful for all the help I could get. It wasn't easy, but with time and patience, my father would slowly begin to heal. He started to slow down on drinking and I took that as a win.

It was a dark and chilly night, and I was walking back home from yet another late shift. As I was walking, I heard a loud howl in the distance. At first, I thought it was just a stray dog, but as I got closer, the howling became louder and more intense. That's when I saw it - a wolf with its foot caught in a trap.

The wolf was howling in pain, and I could see that its paw was bleeding. I knew that I had to help it, but I was scared. It was late at night, and if anything happened to me, no one would find me until tomorrow morning. But I couldn't let the wolf suffer with its bloody paw in the trap.

As I approached the wolf, it appeared to be calm. It looked at me with its big brown eyes, and I could see that it was in a lot of pain. I slowly approached it, trying to be as quiet as possible. The wolf didn't move or growl at me; it just looked at me.

I took a deep breath and reached for the trap. The wolf didn't resist or try to bite me; it just let me take its paw out of the trap. As soon as its paw was free, the wolf got up and disappeared into the darkness.

I stood there for a moment, watching as the wolf ran away. It was a surreal experience - helping a wild animal in need. As I walked back home, I couldn't stop thinking about what had just happened. It was a reminder that we share this world with all kinds of creatures, and sometimes we have to put our fears aside to help them.

The next day, I went back to where I had found the wolf. There were no signs of it or the trap. But I knew that somewhere out there in the wilderness, there was a wolf with a healed paw thanks to my help. It was a small act of kindness, but it made a big difference to that wolf. No one is ever going to believe me about this.

I never thought that my life would change so drastically in a single moment. It was a beautiful summer day, and I was sitting in my room, unwinding from work when I heard a loud knock on the door. I got up to answer it, and that's when I saw my Aunt standing there, tears streaming down her face.

"Kayla, your dad's been in an accident," she said, her voice shaking.

I felt my heart drop into my stomach. My dad? In an

accident? It couldn't be true. But as I looked into my aunt's eyes, I could see the pain and fear there. It was true. We rushed to the hospital, and as we sat in the waiting room, my mind was racing. What had happened? Was he okay? Had he been drinking? Would he be okay? The minutes felt like hours as we waited for news.

Finally, a doctor came out to talk to us. He told us that my dad had been in a car accident on his way home from work. He had suffered some injuries, but they were still assessing the extent of them. They were going to take him into surgery soon.

I felt like I was in a daze as we waited for updates. My Aunt was on the phone with family members, letting them know what had happened. I just sat there, staring at the wall, trying to process everything.

Hours passed before we finally got an update on my dad's condition. He had broken several bones and had some internal injuries. He was stable but still in critical condition. Over the next few days, we spent all our time at the hospital, waiting for my dad to wake up from surgery. When he finally did wake up, it was a relief to see him conscious and talking to us. But he was in a lot of pain, and it was clear that his recovery would be a long road.

As the days turned into weeks, my dad slowly started to get better. He was still in the hospital, but he was able to sit up and talk to us more. We spent a lot of time with him, talking and laughing and trying to keep his spirits up. It was a tough time for all of us, but it brought our family closer together. We realized how much we loved and needed each other, and we were grateful for every moment we had together.

Eventually, my dad was well enough to come home from the hospital. He still had a lot of healing to do, but he was on the road to recovery. It was a long and difficult journey, but we made it through together. The accident changed our lives in so many ways. It reminded us of the fragility of life and the importance of cherishing every moment. But it also showed us the strength and resilience of our family, and how much love and support can help us through even the toughest times. I think this accident was a big wake-up call for him. He realized that his life was heading in a bad direction and agreed to enter into treatment to help with his PTSD. I've never been prouder of him. But secretly I was worried that I wouldn't be able to take care of it. I had savings but I had no idea how long this was going to take.

One warm summer night, I was walking home from my job at the diner. I had taken a shortcut through the woods, hoping to get home faster. But as I walked deeper into the trees, I began to feel uneasy. It was as if something was watching me, following me. I felt uncomfortable but continued on my way.

Suddenly, I heard a rustling in the bushes. I turned around just in time to see a large black wolf emerge from the underbrush. I froze in terror, unsure of what to do.

But then the wolf spoke.

"Hello, Kayla," it said in a deep, gravelly voice.

I stumbled backward in shock. The wolf had spoken to me!

"Don't be afraid," the wolf said. "I'm not here to harm you." I felt skepticism creep into my bones. Had I worked too many doubles too many times? I didn't know what to believe. Was this really happening? Was I dreaming? I had to believe

"I know you've heard stories about my kind," the wolf continued. "But not all skinwalkers are evil. Some of us just want to live in peace."

I listened as the wolf told me about its life as a skinwalker, about how it had learned to control its powers and use them for good instead of evil. I listened as it spoke of its love for nature and its desire to protect it at all costs. As the night wore on, I found myself growing more and more fascinated by the wolf's story. I began to see it not as a monster, but as a fellow creature of the earth.

And then something even more incredible happened - the wolf began to shift and change before my very eyes. Its fur receded, its limbs elongated, and soon it stood before me as a tall, handsome man with piercing blue eyes. "I am not just a wolf," the man said. "I am a skin-walker, and I have the power to shift between forms and I have a gift for you, for your kindness." He opened up his palm revealing a fistful of coins. "I swear on my magic that you will want for nothing."

I stared at him in wonder. I had never seen anything like this before. "Am I dreaming?" I asked weakly. "This is like something out of the movies."

"You can do whatever you want with these coins but always keep one on you. Whenever you are in need, hold the coin and howl at the moon. I will come to find you. You won't even see me most of the time." He passed me the coins and I couldn't get rid of my look of shock. I didn't even know how much these were worth. The man continued to tell me his story, and I found myself growing more and more enamored with him. He was kind, gentle, and wise beyond his years. And when he finally bid me farewell and disappeared into the night. He repeated his instructions and was gone as quietly as he had come.

I grasped the coins in my hand worried about cashing them in but decided to do it first thing in the morning. When I brought them to a shop, they asked where I had found such coins. I told them that a customer had left them as a tip. It turns out that they were very rare and expensive. Just two out of the fistful were enough to pay for not only rehab but his hospital bill as well. I never told my father where I had gotten the money, only that I had been saving. He didn't press me any further than that.

My father had healed and with a lot of work, he became the best version of himself that he could be. Every night since that night, I hold a gold coin and stare up the sky. I thank my lucky stars for helping that wolf. It proved to me that the smallest of kindness can have the biggest of impact. Thank you my wolf friend, I'll never forget you.

———

CONTINUE THE SERIES WITH
INTO THE DARKNESS, VOLUME 2

ABOUT THE AUTHOR

Ethan Hayes grew up in Oklahoma and moved to Texas when he attended Texas A&M. Upon graduation he was hired by Texas Parks and Wildlife and remained there until he retired twenty-two years later. He currently lives in southeast Texas with his wife and two dogs. When he's not spending time enjoying the outdoors and writing, he sips a cold beer on his front porch while listening to Bluegrass music.

———

Send in your encounter story:
encountersbigfoot@gmail.com

ALSO BY ETHAN HAYES

ALSO BY FREE REIGN PUBLISHING